HEARTBEAT :

CONSTABLE IN THE DALE

Nicholas Rhea

Nicholas Rhea

This edition first
published by Accent Press Ltd – 2008

ISBN 9781906373382
First Published in Hardback by
Robert Hale Ltd 1983

Printed and bound in the UK

Cover Design by Red Dot Design

About The Author

Nicholas Rhea is the pen-name of Peter N. Walker, formerly an inspector with the North Yorkshire Police and the creator of the *Constable* series of books from which the Yorkshire TV series *Heartbeat* has been derived.

Nicholas Rhea tells of some of the colourful incidents and eccentric Yorkshire characters encountered by a country constable, stories which provided the basis for the adventures of PC Nick Rowan, played by Nick Berry, in the TV series.

Peter N. Walker is also the author of *Portrait of the North York Moors* and, married with four children, lives in North Yorkshire.

Chapter 1

'Here, there is plenty of gooseberries which makes my
mouth watter.'
MARJORIE FLEMING (1803–11)

VERY FEW AGRICULTURAL SHOWS are devoted entirely to
gooseberries. Those which do specialise in this useful
and wholesome fruit (*Ribes grossularia*) live in a world
of bulging berries and boosted bushes, and they are
given to fierce competition spiced with awesome claims
about the size of their specimens. Perfection is their goal,
and the bigger the better. It was Mrs Beeton, in her
famous cookery book, who said that 'the high state of
perfection to which the gooseberry has here been
brought, is due to the skill of the English gardeners, for
in no other country does it attain the same size and
flavour.' She added that, when uncultivated, the
gooseberry is small and inferior.

Had she visited Aidensfield to view the fruit of a very
select band of berry growers, she would have regarded
their special fruit as colossal, and those of her proud
gardeners as small and inferior. One sometimes wishes
she had lived to view these supreme examples of *Ribes
grossularia.*

It is berries of this kind that prove beyond doubt that
gooseberry-growing is an art; the monsters produced by

the gooseberry societies around England are staggeringly handsome by their shape, size and quality. Each is a true work of art, and to view a modern Aidensfield berry in its natural habitat is indeed a sight to be treasured. Each berry is grown upon a specially nurtured bush, and, when ripe, is about the size of a domestic hen's egg. Some are larger than golf balls, with pulsing veins prominent against their tender and taut skins. When such enormous berries dangle upon their slender stalks, they threaten to topple the tiny parent plant. These bushes are the strong men of the fruit garden, sturdily bearing their precious loads in defiance of weather, wasps and wind.

It is not easy to define the area of greatest gooseberries. There are about eight other societies, most of which are in Cheshire but a strong claimant to be the leader in the field must be the North Yorkshire village of Egton Bridge, a beautiful place lying deep in the Esk Valley. There, the Egton Bridge Old Gooseberry Society was established in AD 1800, and I am privileged to be a member. I was known as a maiden grower until I produced a berry worthy of display among the champions. The annual meeting continues to be held on Easter Tuesday every year, and the annual show of berries is held on the first Tuesday in August, once the day after Bank Holiday. Since the Government messed around with the calendar, Show Day is now held on an ordinary Tuesday. It may be an ordinary Tuesday to many, but it is a very important Tuesday for berry growers.

Before daring to show a berry, I had to familiarise myself with the rules. For example, it is stipulated that all berries handed to the weighman must be sound and dry. Twin berries are defined as those which are two on one stem, grown naturally, and they must be distinctly twins. Furthermore, a pair of twins cannot be split; either both are shown, or none.

The heaviest berry takes the premier prize of the show, and if that happens to be the work of a maiden grower, then he also takes the maiden prize. There are first, second and third prizes for the heaviest twelve berries, and for the heaviest six; the four colours, yellow, red, green and white, attract their own prizes, and hairy ones have their place too.

The rules which govern the taking of berries from other persons' trees are stringent, but the prize-winning fruit are wonderful to behold. A recent winning berry weighed over 1½ ounces; there would be about ten of these berries to a pound. Indeed the World Champion gooseberry was claimed by Egton Bridge for over thirty years, the world champion grower being Mr Tom Ventress, president of the local society. The World Championships have been held at Egton Bridge for nearly 200 years, although the society records only date to 1843. This must surely be the doyen of all gooseberry shows, and it competes with those in distant places like Derbyshire and even Brighton. They are always in the background, while Egton Bridge hogs the stage – that was the situation until the Aidensfield Old Gooseberry Society was founded.

No one quite knew how it started, but reliable sources suggest that someone crept into Egton Bridge one very dark evening and stole several show bushes from the garden of a noted grower. The story says that these were smuggled across the moors and planted in a quiet cottage garden at Aidensfield, where they were fiercely guarded and brought to maturity in secret behind tall fences and a crop of well-regulated nettles.

The story is quite feasible because in Yorkshire it seems that only the Egton Bridge berry bushes are capable of producing the gargantuan fruit so necessary for show purposes. This meant that if the Aidensfield Growers wished to knock the Egton Bridge men off their prickly pedestals, they would require bushes with the same inherent qualities. Such plants rarely grace the *market overt.*

Sometimes, I wonder if those rumours of berry-bush smuggling were circulated to discredit the Aidensfield trees, for it is fair to say that the Aidensfield Society did boast such grandly named trees as Lord Kitchener, Lord Derby, Blücher, Thatcher, Woodpecker, Surprise, Princess Royal and Admiral Beatty, all top names in the gooseberry world. This is quality – it would take a good thief to steal such gems. I suspect it is just a nasty legend.

From those first trees, therefore, by whatever means they arrived, the Aidensfield Society flourished, each new member taking cuttings off the first of its type until a select number of village gardens boasted a veritable forest of thorny competitors.

During the formative years of the Aidensfield Society, the presence of those bushes was a closely guarded secret and it was not until they were producing colossal fruit that they were revealed to an astonished world. It came with the shock announcement that one berry from Aidensfield would be competing in the forthcoming World Championships at Egton Bridge.

The fact that no one, not even the experts, had heard of the Aidensfield gooseberry caused a furore among the other growers. Even those experts from distant parts of England had never wrested the World Championship from the noble Eskdale village, so the first showing of an Aidensfield berry was earth-shattering in its audacity. It was akin to a learner driver in a mini-car competing in the World Motor Racing Championships and I happened to be village policeman at Aidensfield during the run-up to this grim competition.

It transpired that seven residents of Aidensfield owned trees. Every one of them had bush ancestors in the Egton Bridge locality, and each of those seven people had for years protected their berries against unauthorised attention. Their secret had been brilliantly maintained until it was time to execute the coup de grâce.

The President of the Aidensfield Society was Joe Marshall, a retired railwayman who lived in a beautiful cottage along the lane at the eastern edge of Aidensfield. His home stood close to the highway, with an extensive garden behind. It was in the seclusion of that garden that Joe nurtured his berries, and he hailed me from there one fine July morning.

He was a stocky man who habitually wore brown corduroy trousers, a grey sports jacket and black hob-nailed boots. In his late sixties, he sported a flat cap which never left his head, indoors or out, so I never knew whether his iron-grey hair covered his entire head or merely sprouted below the rim of his headgear.

'Mr Rhea,' he announced solemnly, removing a smoking briar pipe from his mouth. 'Ah'm right glad to find you.'

''Morning Joe,' I greeted him. 'Trouble, is it?'

'Nay,' he said slowly in the manner of a Yorkshireman, 'not trouble. Help, Ah think. Guidance, mebbe.'

'Right,' I said. 'How can I help or be of guidance?'

'Thoo'd better come in,' and he led me into the smart, sunny kitchen of his home where his wife worked. Mrs Marshall was a shy woman who rarely went out, except to the post office for her pension and to the shop for

5

groceries, but she smiled at me and Joe said, 'Tea, Mr Rhea?'

'Thanks.' It was a warm afternoon, and a drink was welcome, even if it was a hot one. The kettle sang on an open fire, and within minutes, the silent Mrs Marshall in her flowered pinny produced a brown, earthenware teapot and some china cups. She poured delicious helpings of hot tea, and found a plate full of scones with fresh butter and strawberry jam to smother them. It was marvellous.

During her careful ministrations, Joe chattered about the weather, the animals in the fields and a host of other incidental things, and I allowed him to 'waffle on', as we say in Yorkshire, until he came to the point of his request.

'Mr Rhea,' he said eventually, 'Ah'll come straight to the point,' and he drew on that smelly pipe. 'It's about them gooseberries of mine.'

'Gooseberries?' At this stage, I was blissfully unaware of the forthcoming competition.

'Aye, thoo knaws!'

I didn't know, and the expression of my face must have told him so. 'What gooseberries?' I asked, looking at Joe and his wife for guidance.

'By gum!' he almost shouted. 'Thoo must be t'only feller in these parts that dissn't knaw!'

'Sorry!' I apologised. 'Am I missing something?'

'Thoo'll knaw aboot yon gooseberry show across at Egton Bridge?' He put the question in the form of a statement.

'Yes,' I said, but I didn't inform him that I was a member who qualified as a maiden grower. Obviously, he didn't know about my Yellow Woodpeckers.

'Aye, well, we've set up our own society, and we're

gahin ti beat them Egton Bridgers. We've been growing berries for a few years, allus waiting until our bushes and berries were just right. And now, they are. This year, we're gahin ovver t'moors wiv oor berries, and we'll come back here wi t'World Championship!'

'Does anybody else know about this?' I asked.

'Nay,' he said. 'Nobody, except us seven. Ah was joking, when Ah said thoo should have known. There's just us seven.'

'You seven?' I raised my eyebrows.

'Ah, there's seven of us, all members of this Society. We've kept things very secret because we want to catch them Egton Bridgers napping.'

As he spoke, a feeling of impending horror crossed my mind. As a member of the opposing Society, I could be considered a spy! I was one of the dreaded Egton Bridgers and he didn't know! And he'd laid open his soul to me in a moment of deepest trust. I wondered how the *News of the World* would treat the revelation of a gooseberry spy in Aidensfield.

'What do you want me to do?' My voice quivered as I put my question.

'Guard oor berries,' he said. 'When you're out on patrol, we all want you to look to our bushes.'

'Nobody's going to nobble them, surely?' I put to him, wondering if he'd received some intelligence reports from the Esk Valley.

'Ah wouldn't put it past 'em,' he said, shaking the stem of his pipe at me. 'Ah wouldn't that! If they know we've a world beater on our hands, they might send troops out to stick pins into our fruit, or knock 'em off t'bushes. Ah can't take that sort of a risk, thoo sees, there's a lot at stake.'

My intimate knowledge of the Egton Bridge growers

assured me that they would never stoop to such ploys to beat the opposition. Their inbred confidence and growing ability, plus the secret ways they had with gooseberry bushes, meant there had never been any serious threat to their unique position in the gooseberry world. No one from beyond that lovely village could beat an Egton Bridge grower by fair means. The Eskdale berries would always beat the world, and I knew that the Egton Bridgers would let the Ryedale berries grow in peace. They had no reason to do otherwise – the Egton Bridgers were invincible. Or were they? I dismissed any lingering doubts as pure fantasy!

I tried to convince Joe Marshall of that fact, but knew I was facing a losing battle. He was convinced his berries would be nobbled, so I was compelled to do my duty in the protection of his property, and I reassured him that I would patrol diligently past his gooseberry patch from time to time. I would keep an eagle eye cast for signs of illegal attention to his maturing fruit, and those of his colleagues.

Throughout July, therefore, I maintained my vigil, and I also paid close attention to the six other growers in the village. No one nobbled the growing fruit, and towards the end of July, Joe called me into his home.

'Mr Rhea,' he said, 'Ah's fair capped that thoo's seen fit ti keep an eye on them berries o' mine. They're coming on grand, real whoppers they are. Ah reckon one of 'em might just get that title away from Egton Bridge. Ah'll settle for t'World Championship.'

I didn't like to disappoint him, but none of his berries was anything like the necessary size to achieve that distinction. Certainly they were gigantic by the standards of those seen in any fruit shop or market stall, but by Egton Bridge standards, they were by no means remarkable. 'Nobbut middlin' as they would be described.

'What does thoo think of 'em, then?' he put to me, his pipe issuing thick fumes of astonishing pungency.

'Nice berries,' I said, for I could not say otherwise. Indeed, I had half a dozen on my own bushes which were bigger than any of Joe's. I couldn't deflate the poor old fellow; I let him ride on his wave of optimism.

'This 'ere pipe,' he said, removing it and brandishing it around, 'This 'ere pipe keeps t' wasps off. Ah blows smoke across them berries every day, and it puts a lining on t'berries. It makes wasps keep clear; if they can get near, Mr Rhea, they'll punch a hole in t'fruit to get at t'juice, just like a needle gahin in, and Ah dossn't let that happen. This tobacco smoke keeps 'em off.'

I knew of that trick and I also knew that pigs' blood and cow muck were ideal for manuring the bushes. Joe didn't seem to use those – by his methods trees were surrounded with fireside ashes which he'd spread last autumn to prevent this year's caterpillars climbing up the trees. Some growers put coal dust around the roots in the early spring as a substitute for spraying and there were other tricks too. Joe appeared to know most of them.

He told me how he made little umbrellas of linen to place over the huge berries to prevent heavy rain knocking them off, or causing them to burst by swelling too rapidly. He also fed them with a mixture of sugar and water. Sometimes, when a truly colossal berry made its appearance, the grower would fashion a tiny hammock to sling beneath it. This was to give the straining stalk some relief from its continuing effort to support the bulbous fruit, a sort of berry brassiere.

Joe spent a long time with me. He told me most of his secrets and explained how he'd learned these surreptitiously from a boastful Egton Bridger who had failed to realise that Joe was a future competitor. I wondered if Joe knew my secret ...

My own berries were coming along fine. My little colony of six Yellow Woodpecker bushes was in a sunny but sheltered place in my hilltop garden. Upon them, I had lavished great care and attention of the kind outlined by Joe, expertise I had gleaned from generations of prize growers. My own berries were astonishingly beautiful and round, certainly worthy of the show.

The Egton Bridge show was the day after Bank Holiday Monday; my entry was authorised because of my membership of the Egton Bridge Old Gooseberry Society, but my competing berries must come from my own trees. That presented no problems. They had to be with the weighman before two o'clock on the afternoon of the show, and would remain on the table until seven-thirty that night.

Having been privileged to see the size of Joe's specimens, I began to contemplate entering my own. I did not believe I had a World Champion among my little charmers, but I might just get into the prize list with the heaviest six, or even a single heavyweight in yellow. I began to muse over the possibility. With the end of July, the day of the berry show was almost upon us.

I had to work on that Bank Holiday, performing a motorcycle patrol throughout Ryedale from ten o'clock in the morning until six that evening. My duties entailed stopping the bike in villages to undertake foot patrols, as well as keeping an eye on holiday traffic, seeking thieves who stole from cars in beauty spots and youngsters who used the holiday as an excuse to drink themselves into oblivion in the local hostelries.

All day, my mind was far away, over the moors in

Eskdale, thinking about gooseberries. I could not miss the final opportunity of making a cheeky inspection of Joe's berries, so I parked the faithful Francis Barnett in Aidensfield, close to the village hall, and donned my flat cap instead of my motorcycle crash helmet. I began one of my routine foot patrols; it was mid-afternoon on a hot, sticky August Bank Holiday Monday.

I was in shirt sleeves and hadn't realised how clammy the day had become; the wind from my motorcycle had kept me blissfully cool and unaware of the heat. As I walked along the lane to Joe's house, I felt like sipping a long cool glass of orange squash. The heat was intense.

But Joe didn't believe in such drinks. When he saw me heading towards his garden wall, he called me in and his silent wife produced a mug of her instant tea. I drank it, and the sweat poured out as he walked me about his garden. He still wore his corduroys, jacket, boots and flat cap.

'Just thoo look at yon berries, Mr Rhea,' he eyed them with pride. 'Thoo's done a grand job, protecting 'em like you have, Ah'm grateful.'

'It's all part of the service, Joe,' I said, closely inspecting the berries. One had burst, I noted, and none of the others was up to Egton Bridge standard. I realised I had not seen any of the opposition, except my own little clutch, so perhaps this was a poor berry year? Were the Egton Bridge whoppers smaller than normal?

We would all know tomorrow. I went home and booked off duty. That night I decided to enter the Gooseberry Show.

Next morning, having allowed the hot sun to dry my Yellow Woodpeckers, I picked the largest single berry I could find, and followed with a further six. I packed them gently in an open box of cotton wool, and began the long drive across the spectacular heights of the North Yorkshire moors. The scenery must be seen to be believed; I once met a Londoner who thought the moors were flat, and I wondered if he also believed the moon was a green gooseberry!

I drove into Egton Bridge, parked near the gigantic Catholic Church of St Hedda, and entered the building next door. Many years ago, this used to be the church but it is now the village Catholic School where I learned my reading, writing and arithmetic. On Show Day, it is converted into an arena for displaying monster berries.

I was off duty, of course, and clad in Berry Show clothing which really meant a good suit because members enjoy dinner afterwards, at the curious hour of half-past five, in a local hotel.

I located the small queue near the weighman and joined the growing number, clutching my seven Yellow Woodpeckers in their cosy bed of cotton wool. Each man's berries were carefully weighed and documented before being placed on the table for exhibition, and my large single Yellow Woodpecker weighed in at 20 drams 11 grains, a very useful fruit, but far short of the World Record of 30 drams, 9 grains. The six accompanying berries weighed a total of six ounces, 5 drams and 10 grains, but I would not know whether I was included in any prize list until all had been weighed and catalogued. The beautiful scales used for the ceremony are serviced regularly and they are so delicate that the tiniest feather affects them. The difference between a champion berry and a second best is miniscule in terms of weight, but enormous in terms of prestige.

I turned to leave the weighman's table and bumped straight into Joe Marshall; he stood in the queue bearing a little box which he shielded with his big hands.

'Ah, Joe!' I beamed at him. 'Is that one of your champions?'

'Noo then, Mr Rhea,' he smiled slyly at me. 'Nice day.'

'It's a lovely day, Joe,' I eyed the box, but he kept it covered. 'Is that the world champion then?'

''Appen,' he said.

He was very reticent about revealing the gem he cosseted so carefully, and I suspected something was afoot.

'Summat wrong, Joe?' I asked. 'Has your berry burst, or something?'

'Nay, lad,' he beamed. 'This is a cracker, mark my words,' and he graciously opened his box to reveal a colossal Lord Derby of magnificent proportions.

'By, that's a rare berry!' I spoke with genuine surprise. 'Is it one of yours, Joe?'

'Aye, lad, it is that,' he sounded very smug. I wondered why I had not seen this fruit on any of his Aidensfield trees, and I must admit that I suspected skulduggery of some kind. Had Joe Marshall and his mates done the very thing they'd expected of the Egton Bridgers? Had he raided an Egton Bridge bush to steal this giant?

'It looks like a winner,' I had to admit, for it was certainly bigger than my Yellow Woodpecker.

'Mr Rhea,' he whispered confidentially, 'Sorry about this...'

'Sorry for what, Joe?' I was puzzled.

'The secrecy about this big 'un.'

I didn't understand his remark because my brain was racing to anticipate his next statement.

'Go on,' I said, as others brushed past us to weigh in.

'We cheated thoo a bit,' he admitted. 'We knew thoo

13

was a chap frev this area, and that thoo grew berries for showing.'

'Go on,' I folded my arms and looked steadily at him.

'Well, thoo sees, we reckoned that if we persuaded thoo to look to our bushes, thoo'd see t'quality of oor berries, and then thoo'd tell t'Egton Bridgers they were no good.'

'Go on,' I instructed the crafty character.

'Well, dissn't thoo see? We kept this big 'un very, very secret. Thoo was allowed ti see all oor middling berries, and we reckoned thoo wad tell these folks over here how small oor berries were, then they'd nut bother aboot growing very big 'uns this year ...'

'Joe!' I said, pretending to be hurt. 'You didn't ...'

'Aye, well, we wanted this big chap to be a surprise, thoo sees, to win t'Best in t'Show award ...'

I gazed at the massive berry. Unless someone from Egton Bridge produced a bigger one, Joe's berry might win this year's award. Then I smiled at him.

'Joe,' I said, 'I didn't tell a soul. I didn't report back here – there's no need. These chaps don't stoop to terrible things like nobbling their competitors' berries! They fight true. In fact, I've entered one of my own.'

'Thoo has?' It was my turn to surprise him.

'A Yellow Woodpecker,' I said proudly. 'It's been weighed in, it'll be on the table now.'

He blanched. 'Thoo can't beat this 'un o' mine?' he gasped.

'No,' I smiled. 'But there's more to come from Egton Bridge.'

He weighed-in his prize fruit and it scaled at 25 drams 9 grains, a large berry, and, to be honest, large enough to win the prize for this show, albeit not to gain the World Championship. He had beaten me, but would he triumph

14

over this village of champions?

'Joe,' I asked when he came back to talk to me. 'Where did you grow that berry?'

'In a spot not far from my house,' he smiled. 'Ah kept it very secret, and shall yet. Next year, thoo'll see, Ah'll grow a real big 'un ...'

He checked the time. The latest for weighing-in was two o'clock and it was five minutes to two as we waited. An air of expectancy descended as the final moments ticked away. I could see Joe's crafty face growing redder and redder as he visualised himself walking off with the Champion berry prize for this year. But at the last moment, in walked a pretty woman clutching a jewellery box. She ran across to the table and smiled at the weighman.

'Am I too late?' she oozed at him.

'Nay, lass, thoo's just made it in time,' said the man, accepting her box.

Out of it, she produced a colossal Yellow Woodpecker, and gasps of astonishment filled the room. The crowd surged forward as the enormous fruit was placed delicately on the scales.

'It's from your own tree, is it?' The question had to be asked.

'Yes, my dad gave them to me and I've grown them myself. This is my first try, though, and I don't know if it's any good ...'

As she twittered on, he announced the weight, and the clock struck two.

'Twenty-seven drams, fifteen grains,' came the verdict. 'This is the year's Champion Berry ... Miss Jean Ferris ...'

'She's from Egton Bridge,' I leaned across and smiled at the unhappy Joe. 'You'll have to try harder next time, Joe.'

'I used a recipe given to me by my dad,' said the young woman, 'but he said not to tell anyone what it was...'

Loud applause filled the busy room, as the doors opened to admit the sightseers, and I wondered if she was the first woman to win a berry championship. Maybe she'd try for the World Championship next year?

But as a maiden grower, she'd upheld the reputation of the berry village of the North Yorkshire moors.

If Joe Marshall's dream was to win the World Championship for gooseberries, then Hubert Mitford wanted to raise his status by winning the Best of Breed with his Large White pigs at the Great Yorkshire Show.

Hubert's pigs were certainly noted in Aidensfield, if only because their presence was confirmed by the strong smell which rose from their sties, and by the continuing grunts of satisfaction which filled the evening air at feeding time. Occasionally, one of them would escape to gallop in joy along the main street, or else to sample the culinary delights of the cottage gardens *en route* to freedom out in the big wide world. One frisky piglet got into the pub where it scattered the bar stools and terrified a barmaid in its wild thrashings as it was chased by the assembled drinkers.

But such incidents apart, Hubert's litter of beautiful white pigs was one of the prides of Aidensfield. He carted them to all the local agricultural shows, and came back with rosettes and cups; he bred lovely little pigs and handsome large pigs, and he knew them all by their first names. It seemed they all knew Hubert too, and there was undoubtedly a firm bond of affection between man and beast at Brantgate Farm.

Every time he won at a show, Hubert would visit the Brewers Arms and buy drinks for everyone, local and visitor alike, consequently it was in the interests of the community to ensure Hubert's pigs were the best in Yorkshire. And indeed they were; they thrived on an expert diet of excellent food, personally supervised by Hubert. Among their treats were many delicacies from proud villagers, and he even named his best sows after some of the village ladies. I'm not sure whether they knew that. Everyone wondered who 'Cuddles' really was, for she had beautiful eyes, a fine rump and shapely rear legs with juicy, milky white thighs.

Hubert's popularity in the village and the good will he generated through his wonderful animals led to the vicar deciding to buy a pig. He did so in the belief that his activities would draw people to him as they were drawn to Hubert and thus he would fill his empty pews.

I received my first hint of this when the Reverend Roger Clifton hailed me as I patrolled along the village street.

'Mr Rhea,' he greeted me formally. 'I was hoping to catch you.'

'Yes, Vicar?' I liked him; he was a friendly man who worked hard to preach his faith.

'I am contemplating the purchase of a pig,' he said seriously, 'and wondered whether I need a licence of any kind.'

'You will need a movement licence to bring it from the place of purchase,' I answered, 'so the Ministry of Agriculture can trace its movements should it catch Swine Fever or some other notifiable disease.'

'And where do I get such a licence?'

'From the place you buy the pig,' I said. 'Usually, there is a policeman at the market to issue pig licences.'

'And that is all?'

'So far as I know,' I had to admit. 'Where will you

keep it?'

'There are six disused sties at the vicarage,' he said. 'They are very sound and fully enclosed with a brick wall. I'll use those.'

I did not know whether any recent legislation had imposed conditions about keeping pigs on private premises, and advised him to discuss this with the Ministry of Agriculture or the local council. After talking about the village and its flock, he went on his way rejoicing, and I popped into the Brewers Arms for one of my routine official visits.

Two weeks later, the Rev. Roger Clifton journeyed along the village street, beside the driver of a Land-Rover which towed a trailer. In that trailer was a delightful Large White sow. The parish had acquired a pig.

The Parochial Church Pig was one of his undoubted hits. She was christened White Lily, which means purity and modesty, a fitting name for an unmarried sow. As the lovely creature blossomed in the fullness of her youth, and flourished on her diet of holy scraps with lashings of mashed potato, she found herself being used as the basis for many sermons. All kind of parallels were suggested from the pulpit, and the swine of biblical times became succulent meat for the Rev Roger Clifton.

I think Mr Clifton, in truth, had rejected any suggestion of ever killing the fat pig because he often quoted those parts of the Scriptures where the meat of the pig was not to be eaten because it was considered unclean. This was not a nice thing to say of White Lily, and he reminded his congregation of the Hebrews' views on the subject when he said, 'It is said they held the flesh of this animal in such detestation, that they would not so much as pronounce its name, but instead of it said, "The beast, that thing".' The village felt he did this to gain sympathy for White Lily, and so it became evident that the vicar had no intention of killing Lily or of selling her on the market. So, instead of White Lily helping to swell the Parochial Church Funds, she became another mouth to feed on the Parochial Church Income.

One village gossip, a voluble lady, who felt the church shouldn't subsidise a pig, said that the Hebrews and Phoenicians only abstained from pork because there was none in their country, but the vicar retaliated by quoting from the Book of Proverbs, Chapter 11, Verse 22, where it said, 'As a jewel of gold in a swine's snout, so is a fair woman without discretion.' No one really understood it, except that it meant the church pig was not for sale.

I think it was another villager's quote from Matthew, Chapter 8, Verse 30, about a herd of swine feeding, that gave the vicar an idea. He would keep the sow and breed from her. He would produce a litter of swine, and sell the little ones. That would satisfy his critics, for church funds would swell to enormous proportions. At least, that was the Rev. Clifton's theory.

By chance, some time later, I was in Hubert Mitford's farmyard, leaning on a pigsty wall with a coffee in my hand as the Reverend Roger arrived. He had come to discuss the possibility of breeding a litter of pigs from White Lily.

At that stage, I had no idea of his plan, but his blushing hesitancy suggested he wished to talk about a delicate matter.

'I'll go,' I said, diplomatically.

'No, Mr Rhea, don't go on my account.' He shook his head vigorously. 'I'd like you to hear my plans.'

'Summat good, is it?' smiled Hubert, revelling in the

Reverend's shyness.

'That sow of mine, Hubert,' the vicar took a deep breath and spoke his piece. 'I'm thinking of breeding from her.'

'Ah!' beamed the farmer with an evil glint in his eye. 'Then that'll be more pigs for t'church to keep.'

'No,' cried the vicar. 'No, it won't. You see, I will keep White Lily, and sell her piglets. I was wondering whether this was feasible ... I don't know much about pig-breeding, you see ...'

'Ah've a smashing awd boar,' came in Hubert, 'Nobbut a tenner a time for serving a sow. If that's what thoo's come for, Vicar, Ah'm your man. Ah'll soon fix yon pig and she'll give nice little piglets that'll sell like hot cakes at Thirsk Mart.'

'Is there a special time, then?'

'Well, noo, there might be and there again there might not,' smiled Hubert. 'Ah'll tell thoo what, Vicar. Ah'm summat of an expert in these matters, so Ah'll pop around to see that pig o'thine, and we'll soon get her fettled up.'

The vicar looked at me.

'Well, Mr Rhea? Do you think it will make money for my church?'

I had to be honest and say I did. Many folks who had taken to breeding pigs had made money, so I gave my considered view that the church at Aidensfield was about to prove yet again that where there's muck, there's money.

It would be three weeks later when I saw the Reverend Roger taking his pig to be served by a boar. In the manner of a medieval monk, he had a long piece of rope tied to one of White Lily's hind legs and she was ambling down the street, sampling the growth of the verges and causing ladies to leap for safety into houses and gardens. This contented pig grunted and rooted until she arrived at Hubert's farm.

There, with the aid of Hubert's skill, she was driven towards a cosy pen for a hectic session of love-making with one of his prize boars. There could be no doubt that White Lily's litter would be beautiful and valuable, and in that sense, Hubert was doing more than his bit for the church.

As I was there, I helped to drive White Lily through the gate, and was a witness to the next, and most important, part of the proceedings.

Hubert brought the boar from a sty; he was a massive, ugly creature but he must have been a prince in a white suit in the eyes of the waiting maiden because she grunted with gleeful expectation as the scent of his ardour reached her nostrils. Hubert opened the gate and the willing boar needed no further guidance; he was beside his loved one in a trice, sniffing with pleasure at the perfume she wore.

Hubert shut the gate. They were alone.

At this stage, the pink, embarrassed complexion of the Reverend Roger turned a brilliant red. He had, by some mischance, positioned himself very close to the marital bed and was clearly embarrassed by the opening sounds and visions of pleasure coming from the happy couple.

'Er, Hubert,' he said, 'I've never been in this position before ... I mean, do I have to observe the actual ... er ... the ... coupling ... I mean, it is parish funds that are being used for this ... er ... enterprise ... Do you think I should wait and see that they ... er ... do it properly?'

'Aye,' said Hubert, 'thoo'd better, 'cos thoo won't have time to marry 'em.'

And so the story had a happy ending. The pigs got

married and lived happily for a few minutes, and in time White Lily produced eight lovely piglets. The parish was happy at this event and brought even more food for their pigs. I believe the church made a handsome profit from its first year of breeding. Today, if you go down the side of the vicarage, you can still hear the descendants of White Lily and her various beaus, as they grunt and snuffle around the vicarage gardens, raising much needed funds for the faithful of Aidensfield.

But for Hubert, things did not work out quite so well.

Through his important contacts in the pig world, and due to his standing in the village, Hubert decided to offer himself for election to the Rural District Council. He sincerely felt he had a great deal to offer society in general, and the folk of Aidensfield in particular, and so he sought, and achieved, nomination as the official candidate for that ward. But there was one terrible problem associated with his nomination. He had decided to stand as a Liberal.

This was shattering news. Never in the political history of the area had a Liberal emerged from anywhere to stand at any election, national or local. Horror was expressed at his decision; Hubert's standing slumped and there were fears about his sanity. Indeed, there were also fears about the future of the church's pig-breeding enterprise. Could a Liberal be allowed access to this capitalist venture? For years, nay centuries, the folk of this blissful rural area had always voted Conservative; Churchill and his men were for Britain, and any other political adherent was deemed a dangerous subversive.

Heaven knows what might have happened if Hubert had opted for Socialism, for there would have been worries about nationalisation of the pig-breeding enterprise or whether the Red Flag would be sung in church. As he had opted for Liberalism, however, such events were unlikely, but his new-found creed meant that no one really knew what he stood for. This meant he could canvass around the district without fear of contradiction, and this lack of contradiction made him believe his policies were acceptable. The truth was that no one argued because no one understood his policies.

Inevitably, election day arrived. The school was used as the polling station, and I had to perform a long day's duty, from seven o'clock in the morning to the close of polling at 10 p.m. My duty was to ensure there were no election offences or breaches of the Representation of the People Act, 1949. I had to make my presence obvious around the polling station, looking fierce and making sure no one used undue influence or threatened any force during the voting. I had to ensure that no bribery was used and that no one voted in the name of any other person. Order had to be maintained throughout and I made friends with the Returning Officer because she was pretty and had brought a kettle.

After my early start, the day wore on, and I noticed that Hubert had really immersed himself in the occasion. He wore a massive yellow rosette and had decorated his old car with yellow banners as he trundled it around outlying farms and houses to convey his supposed voters to the polling booth. I knew they wouldn't vote for him; a free ride was fine, but voting Liberal was something no one would do.

But I had to admire Hubert. He never gave up. He chattered to potential voters, made countless trips in his car, and gave yellow rosettes to everyone. And all the time he tried to convert rock-hard Conservatives to his new faith.

At ten o'clock, prompt, the polls closed and my job was to oversee the sealing of the ballot boxes, following which I had to escort them to a collecting centre at the council offices. There, the count would take place. *En route,* we collected many more boxes from other villages and I signed a form to say none had been tampered with.

I got home around quarter past midnight, and was just sitting down for a hot goodnight drink when my telephone rang. Mary dashed through to answer it before it roused the children, and said, 'It's Hubert, he sounds upset.'

'The results won't be out yet!' I remarked as I trudged through to the telephone.

I picked up the handset. 'P.C. Rhea,' I announced.

'Mr Rhea, thoo'll have to cum quick. Real quick.' I recognised the urgency in Hubert's voice.

'What's matter?' I put to him.

'It's my pigs,' he said. 'I reckon they've caught summat real bad, and wondered if it needed reporting. They look terrible ...'

'Have you called the vet?' I asked.

'He's not in yet, he's out at Brantsford with a calving cow.'

'I'll be there in five minutes,' I assured him.

Not knowing a great deal about contagious diseases of animals, I nonetheless knew that I would have to do something quickly, so I gulped down my cup of cocoa and hurried on foot towards his farm.

When I arrived, his car, still bearing the yellow banners and flags, stood in the foldyard. Several placards in dazzling yellow stood around the walls, but on the ground the mud was brown and thick. I splodged across to his sties and found him standing near the end wall, looking dejectedly at the pigs inside. As I approached, he heard my squelchy arrival.

'Ah, Mr Rhea, thoo's come then.'

I halted at his side.

He shone a powerful torch into the sty, and there, grunting in the dazzling light, were a dozen glowing pigs. They looked terrible.

'Are they all like that, Hubert?' I asked.

'Aye,' he said sadly.

Then I laughed. 'Hubert!' I almost cried with laughter, 'They're not ill! Somebody's turned them all into little Liberals, that's all!'

Every one of them had been sprayed with a bright yellow paint.

Next day, it was announced that Hubert had polled four votes, and we never knew who'd perpetrated any of those deeds.

Chapter 2

'Ah, when will this long weary day have end, And lend
me leave to come unto my love?'
EDMUND SPENSER (1552–99)

THIS IS THE STORY of a man called Soldier, and because
he spent some of his time in prison I will refer to him by
that name alone. He was known affectionately as Soldier
during his incarceration, and although he lived at
Brantsford I first met him at a police station on the south
coast of England. It happened like this.

Sergeant Blaketon rang me late one evening at the
latter end of summer, and said, 'Rhea, there's an escort
job for you. Catch the first train from York tomorrow
morning, and go to Brighton, there's a prisoner to fetch
back. Foxton will go with you. He's got the money for
your fares, the warrant and something for a meal on the
way. I've rung Brighton – they're expecting you. Make
sure the fellow is handcuffed to one of you all the way
back. He's for court at Eltering later this week.'

Sergeant Blaketon gave me the prisoner's name, and
rang off. I called Alwyn Foxton at Ashfordly Police
Station and confirmed what the sergeant had told me. It
seemed our train left shortly before seven o'clock, and
we had to travel in civilian clothes in order to be very
inconspicuous. Alwyn would collect me in the morning
at six o'clock and would have the necessary warrant to

secure Soldier's arrest by our good selves. There were times when such formalities were necessary.

Everything was arranged, and so I rose from the warmth of my marital bed at quarter past five next morning to make myself a cooked breakfast. I didn't disturb Mary or the children as I went about stocking my body with hot food, and I had the sense to make sandwiches and provide myself with a flask of coffee for the long trip. Police know from bitter experience that it is wise to arm oneself with food and drink when away from one's usual source of supply. Prompt at six, Alwyn arrived in the official car, and we drove through the wilds of Ryedale to York's famous railway station.

Alwyn Foxton was a jolly, red-faced policeman of indeterminate age, whose thick grey hair and stock figure made him something of a father-figure, even to young constables like myself. Easy-going and affable, he had never sought promotion and was happy to let the big wide world pass gently by. On a long, boring train journey like this, he was good company as he reminisced about his life in the force, and offered words of home-spun wisdom to his youthful colleague.

We reached Brighton before lunch, tired and hungry, and decided to buy some food in town before presenting ourselves at the local police station to collect Soldier. I liked Brighton, except for the beach whose stony slopes are like river beds, and on impulse bought a postcard depicting a pretty part of the resort and posted it home to my mother. I learned afterwards that when she received this missive, hearing the words 'Having a lovely time, Nick,' she thought I'd abandoned my wife, family and career to run away to a new life in the deepest south. Such is the penalty for warped senses of humour, however light the act! We spent some time in the town, rather than wait with a prisoner for our return train, and eventually Alwyn and I entered the door of the police station and made our identities known to the sergeant. It was late afternoon by this time, and we had seen the delights of this lovely town.

The sergeant had difficulty understanding our strange tongue, but after showing him the magistrates' warrant and our warrant cards, he realised we had come to relieve him of Soldier.

He spoke to us in a strange accent and waved his arms, which we interpreted as a request to follow him into the cells. This we did, and Alwyn passed me the handcuffs.

'He's yours,' he said, and I accepted the handcuffs before I realised what responsibilities I had thus acquired. If Soldier escaped, I would be responsible and liable to disciplinary action.

'Cell No. Two,' chanted the sergeant, and we halted at the locked door. He rattled his bunch of keys in the lock and the heavy studded door swung open on well-oiled hinges to reveal a tousle-haired man sitting on the wooden platform which was his bed.

He stood up as we entered.

'Great!' he said, 'Now I can get home.'

'Listen first,' the sergeant ordered him. 'These officers have come to arrest you for failing to answer to your bail.'

'I know,' the man said, 'and I'm not arguing. I just want to go home, that's all.'

'Read the warrant to him,' the sergeant ordered, and Alwyn began a pompous recital of the obscure wording of the document in his hands. In simple terms, it ordered us to arrest Soldier and take him to Eltering Magistrates' Court where he would be dealt with for an offence of housebreaking, committed many months ago. Soldier listened, and shuffled uneasily, wanting only to be out of the cell.

He was a tall man in his middle twenties, with brown hair all tousled and curly; his face, with its hint of freckles and dark brown eyes, bore that unmistakable aura of mischief, and yet it was a friendly face. He was casually dressed in grey trousers and a matching sweater, but his other possessions were in a locker labelled 'Prisoner's property'.

We walked him from the cell into the charge room, where the sergeant formally handed over his belongings, for which he had to sign an official form. There was a small amount of cash, a roll of bedding tied around the middle with a leather belt, a small suitcase and an overcoat.

Our train left at shortly after five and after a farewell cup of tea for us all, the sergeant arranged a car to convey us to the railway station. I asked Soldier to stretch out his arm, and promptly fastened the handcuffs upon him. Having seen that he was right-handed, I fastened the cuffs around his right wrist, so they linked with my left. And so we were handcuffed together with this small, but often valid, precaution. Alwyn folded the warrant, endorsed it as being executed and slid it back into his pocket.

Soldier, and indeed ourselves, were now ready to return to Yorkshire.

We found an empty compartment on the train and jostled ourselves into a comfortable position on the seat, with me sitting by the window and Soldier linked to me by the handcuffs. Since leaving the police station, he had not spoken a word, nor had he offered any resistance. He sat by my side, as good as gold, and watched the passing scenery of Sussex as we gathered speed on our long, tiring journey to the north.

Alwyn sat opposite; he had bought a few magazines and paperbacks for us, offering a glossy magazine to our prisoner. Soldier accepted it with a ready grin, and bowed his head to read.

I did likewise. Within minutes, we found it necessary to reach a neat reading arrangement because, at first, every time he moved his hand to turn a page, I had to lift mine to go with him, and the reverse happened when I wanted to turn a page. We soon got a system working, as Alwyn sat unmoved with his book. Then Soldier began to speak.

'Now we're out of that bloody place,' he said, 'I can talk. You are Yorkshiremen, aren't you? I like Yorkshiremen, coppers or not.'

'We are,' I spoke for both of us.

'Good, then you'll see sense. My name's Soldier. They called me Soldier inside, 'cos of the way I walk. Soldier this, and Soldier that. I did the tobacco baron bit inside, fixed things for the others, you know. Got the screws to unbend a bit, made life easier. They liked me, the others did. Captain of the cricket eleven I was, just because I come from Yorkshire. They don't know how to play cricket do they, those who live outside Yorkshire? I taught 'em a thing or two, with my googlies and off-breaks ...'

And so he rambled on, spilling out the words in a rich tapestry of mixed prison jargon and a Yorkshire accent. I listened enthralled, but Alwyn pretended to continue reading, although I knew he was listening. But Alwyn was not going to admit being tricked into anything ridiculous like listening to the half-truths of a convicted prisoner. But I found myself warming to this voluble man.

'What are you in for?' I asked.

'Passing dud cheques,' he grinned, 'Lots of 'em. I had

a real time, I tell you.'

'In Yorkshire was it?'

'No, all over. Well, you know how it is, Constable. The job got me down, there's the wife and a kid and no money. All work and worry … it just got me down. So I nicked a cheque book and had a bloody good spend.'

'They caught you?'

'In time. I nicked a few more cheque books and stayed at posh hotels. Bought a car an' all, and sold it. Easy money it was, Constable. Dead easy. Better 'n working. Too easy, really. I got daft.'

'What is your job – when you're working?' I put to him.

'Labouring. Building sites and that. Mucky work, heavy sometimes.'

'So they caught you. Who caught you?'

'Liverpool police. I was in this flat, and they found out it was me. Raided the place and caught me with the cheque book. I got sent down for eighteen months. I've done a year, behaved myself, so they've let me out.'

'And now you'll be going straight?' I smiled.

'I am, honest. No, I mean it. You know what I wanted in there? All that time?'

'No.' I let him tell his tale.

'A tea party at my own house. I wanted to get home, see the wife and my little lass, and have a proper tea with a white cloth and nice cups. That's what I've wanted all along. Tea like that, done proper.'

'And your wife? She'll be waiting for you?' I visualised the happy domestic scene.

'Yeh,' he said with some nonchalance, 'Yeh, she will. I wrote you see, said I was coming home today and told her to put a white cloth on.'

'Did she say she'd look forward to it?' as we chatted,

31

I warmed to this likeable fellow.

'She hasn't replied.' There was a suggestion of sadness in his voice. 'Mind you,' he added, 'she wouldn't have time to write back. I mean, they didn't tell me I was going home till a couple of days back, and then I wrote straight away so she'll have just got my letter ...'

'But this arrest? You knew we'd be coming?'

'Oh, aye, I knew that. I didn't answer bail for something way back – housebreaking I think – and the screws said you fellers would be waiting with that warrant. They brought me here. I didn't mind – I mean, I get a free trip home under arrest, and I was going anyway. I'm dying for Yorkshire, you know, I really am. Just dying to see my wife and our kid ...'

'And that white table-cloth?' I smiled.

'Aye, and that.'

Unwittingly, we had caught a slow train to London, and during that journey, Soldier chattered to us like a friend. He was so open, so friendly, so in love with his wife and child, whose name I learned was Susie. He told us of his wishes, his loves, his pranks and dodges in prison, and his escapades with the stolen cheque books. As he chattered, Alwyn Foxton joined in, now relaxing in his role as senior police officer in charge of our prisoner.

'I'm not going to run, you know,' Soldier said eventually. 'You can take those cuffs off.'

Automatically, I glanced down at the chromium plated chain that linked us. There were no passengers in our compartment and Alwyn sat opposite. Soldier's only way of escape would be to jump through the window and risk death by falling on to the line or alternatively to make a dash for the corridor. Both were unlikely.

I made the decision to release him.

'No funny business then!' I said rather inanely.

'Don't be bloody silly, Constable,' he said, 'I'm

going home. I want to go home, don't I?'

I didn't answer, but located the handcuff key in my pocket and loosened the cuffs. I removed them and slid them into my pocket. Alwyn looked askance at me, but said nothing. After all, Soldier was my responsibility. He rubbed his wrist and said, 'Now that's better. I'm not going to run, you know. I won't – honest. There's no need.'

Somehow, I believed him. He produced a paperback from his bag and began to read.

'Agatha Christie,' he said. 'Good stuff, eh?'

And he lapsed into a long reading session. At various stations along the route, people entered and left our train, some joining us in the compartment but none guessing we were two police officers escorting a prisoner north for a court appearance.

Due to the slowness of our train, we were very late arriving at Victoria, and as we slowed at the end of that part of the journey, Soldier put his book away and asked the time.

I remember telling him, although I cannot recall the precise time save to say that Soldier said, 'Then we've twenty minutes to get across London. Our train home goes in twenty minutes, Constable. If we miss it, we won't get home until the early hours.'

'We can't make it across London in twenty minutes!' Alwyn cried.

'We can – I know the way!' chirped Soldier.

'There's tickets to get at the tubes,' I said, 'there's always a queue at the windows ...'

This was before the days of those handy ticket machines, but Soldier said, 'You don't need tickets in the tubes if you've got British Rail tickets. Just show ours – they'll do.'

'Will they?' I asked.

'Course!' he cried, 'Bloody hell, Constable, you've not been around, have you?'

'No,' I admitted. 'Not a lot.'

'Then leave it to me …' he said, 'I'll get us on to that train.'

'I'll have to handcuff you through Victoria,' I said.

'No need,' he assured me, 'I'm not leaving you blokes. You've got my ticket, remember?'

'I can't let you walk through London without them!' I began to worry about this.

'Walk? Who's going to walk, Constable? Run you mean, run like hell. We run like hell, me leading and you chasing. If you don't, we miss that bloody train home, and I don't want to wait until the early hours. I want my bed tonight, and my wife and little girl, and that white tea cloth … I'm going to get all that, mate. All of it. And soon.'

The train was slowing on its final yards and Soldier was on his feet, waiting at the door and clutching his belongings.

'Come on!' he said, 'there's no time to hang about. Keep with me, and don't get left behind. If I lose you,' he said, 'I'll see you at King's Cross barrier … I can get through the tubes all right … don't need tickets if you know the ropes …'

'I'd better just put these on …' I pulled out the cuffs and dangled them before him.

'No time,' he said, 'Come on, lads, run!'

And as the train slowed to its grinding halt, he opened the door and leapt on to the platform before the train halted. He was galloping towards the ticket barrier, shouting for us to follow him, Alwyn was coughing and spluttering and I was dithering.

'You've done it, Nick!' he cried, 'That was a bloody stupid thing to do … he's away … he's a con man, you know … that's you and me for the high jump …'

But I was already jumping from the train in advance of the other passengers and galloping after Soldier. He saw me, waited a moment, and waved urgently.

'Come on!' he shouted. 'Don't hang about.'

Alwyn gathered his wits and we all passed through the barrier together, flashing our tickets. Soldier darted off again, rushing through the crowded station at Victoria and heading for the nearest tube. We followed, Alwyn puffing with advancing age and me desperately trying to keep Soldier in view.

He kept looking behind and waiting for us; he knew exactly where he was going, and we had no alternative but to run with him. Already, he could have escaped and ruined our careers, so we simply galloped through London's crowds with my eye on the back of his bobbing head.

To this day, I cannot remember which way we took. Not being accustomed to London, its web of tube stations and the crowds of stolid-faced humans, I simply followed Soldier and shouted at Alwyn to keep pace. Barrier after barrier was crossed, escalator after escalator was galloped up or down, crowds were parted and people apologised to, and then, as if by magic, we were rushing across the platform at King's Cross.

'Two minutes to go,' Soldier smiled. 'Not bad.'

We hurried along the platform, seeking an empty compartment, but every one was full. People were even standing in the corridors, and as the guard looked at his watch, we opened the nearest door and leapt aboard, panting and perspiring.

'My God!' said Alwyn, 'I never thought we'd all get

here.'

'Me neither,' beamed Soldier, 'I thought you blokes were going to let me down.'

We laughed, and settled down for a long haul home in a crowded corridor. The guard looked at his watch.

'One minute,' grinned Soldier, and at that precise instant, a newsvendor walked down the platform with one or two papers still in his satchel. Like lightning, Soldier dived for the door, opened it and leapt on to the platform.

'Get him!' shouted Alwyn.

But I couldn't move. There was a fat woman directly in front of me, and the guard was shouting and blowing a whistle. I watched with horror as our prisoner galloped up the platform, but he halted before the newsvendor, handed over a coin for a paper and raced back to the open carriage door. Even as the train began to move, he leapt inside, slammed the door and gave the two-fingered sign to the harassed guard.

'Sorry about that,' he said, 'I like a read when I'm on a train,' and opened the London *Evening Standard.*

I breathed a sigh of relief, but daren't look at Alwyn. My poor heart must have missed many beats.

At the first stop, seats became vacant, and we took our places in a crowded compartment, Soldier remaining silent as he studied every word in the paper. I grew increasingly tired and felt like dropping off to sleep, but knew I must not do so. After all, I did have responsibilities.

It was a long, tiring and boring journey with many halts. Soldier solved his boredom by falling asleep but left his paper to be shared by Alwyn and myself.

We were due into York around midnight, so far as I remember, and we were all tired, hungry and travel stained. As we neared the city, I nudged Soldier into wakefulness.

'Come on, Soldier,' I said, 'Get ready to leave. We're coming into York.'

'Then you'd better handcuff me,' he said. 'The sergeant wouldn't like to see me loose like this, would he?'

'No,' I said, thankful he'd reminded me. Having organised ourselves for disembarkation, I slipped the heavy cuffs around his wrist, locked them securely, and smiled at the reaction of our travelling companions. I didn't offer any explanation – they would come to their own conclusions about us, I'm sure.

At York, we left the train and walked sedately along the platform where the tall, gaunt figure of Sergeant Oscar Blaketon awaited. He looked grim and forbidding, but relaxed as he noticed our little party.

'Ah, Foxton and Rhea. You made it then?'

'Yes, Sergeant,' I said.

'No problems with him?'

'None, Sergeant,' I confirmed.

'Right, the car's waiting outside,' and so we were marched through the final barrier. Soldier and I climbed into the waiting police car to be driven home by Oscar Blaketon while Alwyn brought the other car home. Sergeant Blaketon seemed to think there was safety in numbers.

Until this point, Soldier had not spoken to the sergeant, but once we were settled in the car, handcuffed together in the rear seat, Soldier asked, 'Is my wife waiting for me, Sergeant?'

'Wife? No,' he said, expressing surprise at the question.

'Didn't she come to say she'd be surety for me, for my bail?'

'No,' said Blaketon equally bluntly, 'nobody's been.'

'You'll go and ask them for me, won't you?' he addressed the sergeant, leaning forward from the rear seat.

'Rhea can go round when we get to Brantsford.'

Without a surety for bail, he would have to spend his time in our cells until his court appearance. I could see his world beginning to crumble. I could see his precious dream fading, and felt terribly sorry for him.

We arrived at Brantsford Police Station and placed him in the cells. It would be just after one o'clock in the morning, but I went around to his home address to see if his wife was there.

I knocked but got no reply. I peered through the windows, but the house looked deserted. And there was no white cloth on the table.

I had to go back and break the news.

'Sergeant,' I said, 'could I act as surety for him?'

'You, Rhea? Don't be silly,' was Blaketon's response, and so I went home.

Next morning, Mary listened to my story and said, 'Well, bring him here for tea. I'll put a white cloth on.'

I found an excuse to visit Brantsford Police Station that afternoon, and learned his case was due for hearing at Eltering the following morning. Among the other outstanding crimes, he was to be charged with yet another case of false pretences, and I went to see him.

I stood at the cell door, where I spoke through the small square hole in the heavy woodwork.

'Any luck?' I asked.

'No,' he said. 'She's not been.'

'You can come to our house for tea,' I said. 'When this is all over, give me a call, and my wife will put a white cloth on for you. I mean it, Soldier. I owe you a favour.'

'Thanks,' he said, and I noticed the merest hint of a tear in his eye. 'Yeh, thanks. I will. They'll send me down again, you know. I'd have done it willingly, if I could have spent last night at home ... with the wife ... and Susie ...'

'I know,' I said. 'Sorry.'

'Nice to have met you, Constable.'

'I'm at Aidensfield,' I said. 'Rhea's the name.'

'I'll look you up, honest,' he said.

And I left.

He was sentenced to another twelve months imprisonment for his outstanding offences and he never called for his tea. To this day, I do not know what happened to him, but I never saw him at his own house, nor did I ever see his wife and child.

But I will never forget that gallop through London, hard on the heels of my prisoner. So much could have gone wrong, but everything went right because a Yorkshireman wanted a cup of tea and cakes on a white table-cloth with his wife and baby.

There is little doubt that hardened law-breakers do respond to thoughtfulness and kindness from police officers. I was given a perfect example of this late one Saturday night during a noisy dance at Ashfordly Town Hall.

The dance attracted many lively youngsters from neighbouring market towns and villages, and I was drafted into Ashfordly that night to increase the strength of the local force. My presence made it two constables on duty that night – two against about 250 revellers.

There was the usual noise and loud music from the hall as the dance was in full swing, but little or no trouble. If there was to be a problem, it would start as the local pubs turned out, when young men, full of fiery liquid, attempted to show who was the best at whatever caught their fancy. Much of it would be a show of bravado richly combined with stupidity, for such antics generate a lot of noise but little else. High spirits at this level can be tolerated.

As the pubs closed their doors, therefore, Alwyn Foxton and I separated and patrolled the town to reveal the presence of our dark blue uniforms in strategic places. In those days, the police uniform was respected, and it did not encourage trouble; many of the noisy youths simply continued their noise but did not reduce themselves to fighting. Instead they formed a modest procession from the pubs into the dance hall, filling it almost to capacity.

Once they were inside, we could breathe a sigh of relief. When the majority were indoors Alwyn and I slipped into the caretaker's office for a welcome cup of tea. It was now 11 p.m.; the dance ended at quarter to midnight, and we reckoned to have the market square clear by the stroke of twelve.

We did not prolong the cup-of-tea break; within ten minutes, I was heading for the stairs which climbed to the dance floor, my purpose being to poke my nose through the door of the hall to show the uniform yet again. Such periodical displays of our dark blue suits did achieve results. These dances generated very little trouble.

But as I climbed the stairs, a pretty girl of about twenty in a delightful blue dress called me and her voice had a note of urgency.

'Mr Rhea!' She knew my name; I recognised her as a girl called Sandra who worked in a local shop. 'Mr Rhea, quickly, up here.'

She turned and raced up the stairs, her slim legs and swaying body being enough to make the most sluggish of hearts miss a beat or two. I followed, trotting in her wake until she paused outside the gents' toilet.

'In there,' she said.

'Trouble?' I asked, panting after my race up the stairs.

'My boyfriend,' she said. 'He's hurt.'

And as I entered the toilet area, I noticed large drops of blood on the wooden floor. Fresh blood. I could see a trail of it along the landing and into this toilet; it led from the rear staircase. I had no idea what to expect.

Inside, I found him.

A scruffy, long-haired and rather surly youth was sprawled across the two washbasins, one of them taking his weight while the other, with its running cold tap, was full of brilliant red blood made brighter because it was mixed with the flowing water.

He was alone; only his girl hovered outside as I approached.

'Now then,' I said inanely, 'What's happened?'

'Oh,' he stood up, clutching his wrist with the uninjured hand, 'Oh, I fell' he said. 'It's cut bad.'

He kept his bleeding hand over the washbasin as the swirling water carried away the lost blood; the fact that it was bright red blood stirred memories of my First Aid training and I knew it came from an artery, not a vein. He was bleeding profusely and this was no ordinary cut. I noticed the display of agony and worry on his pale face.

'Let me see,' I took hold of his wrist and turned his hand palm upwards so that I could see it, making sure it did not spill on to the floor. Due to the blood welling from the wound, I could not see it clearly, so, gently I returned his hand to the tap to wash away the fountain of blood. And there, right across the palm of his hand, was a long, clean cut almost like a slash from the blade of a sword. It was a clean, but deep and severe wound.

This would need rapid treatment; it required more than first aid or the botched-up bandaging of an amateur of any kind. This lad required urgent and professional medical care.

'You said you fell?' I said, attempting to stem the flow by finding a pressure point.

'Yeh,' he said, assuming something of a cocky air.

'Where?' I was desperately trying to find a pressure point in his arm, searching in the requisite places beneath his biceps or near his wrist.

'Down the steps,' he said vaguely. I knew he was lying. No fall could produce such a clean cut, unless he had fallen on to a knife or some glass. But there was no time to waste investigating his claims; I had to find a doctor. I don't think the lad realised the danger he was facing as his life-blood was being swilled down that sink, being pumped out of his body by his youthful heart.

'Stand still,' I said. We were now attracting an audience. Some of his friends had arrived, and his girl still hovered near the door, her face showing genuine concern but her upbringing keeping her out of the gents' toilet.

'You all right, Kev?' asked a huge, unruly looking ruffian.

'Cut hand,' said my patient. 'Leave us be, the cop's doing his best.'

'You're not taking him in, are you?' came the question.

'I'm taking him to a doctor,' I said. 'This cut needs expert attention.'

'All right, Kev?' His pals sought Kev's agreement to my course of action.

'Yeh,' said Kev, and they slowly dispersed, leaving the worried girl, and myself with the pale youth.

'Ah!' I had found the pressure point beneath his biceps and squeezed tightly. 'Can you hold your own arm there?' I asked him.

'What for?'

'To stop that blood coming out of your hand. You can do it better than me, because we're going to the doctor. Just grip your arm like this,' and I demonstrated the correct method, 'and that'll stop the blood gushing out.'

Holding his injured hand in the air, Kev searched until he found the pressure point, then squeezed hard. He was a fit youth, with the powerful hands of a labourer, and his left hand gripped his own arm and he watched with some fascination as the blood ceased to flow.

'Have you a clean handkerchief?' was my next question.

'I have.' Sandra had now ventured into the toilet and she produced a large white handkerchief from her handbag.

'Good. Now, Kev,' I used the name I'd heard his pals call him. 'I'm going to put this over the cut, right? Just close your fist lightly, and hold it in place. Don't squeeze. Got it?'

His hand closed over the rolled up handkerchief which rapidly changed colour to a brilliant red, and with Kev holding his own brachial pressure point, I escorted him out of the building. Sandra came with us, worried and anxious about him, but I now reassured them that the matter was under control.

As we walked between the cars parked in the market place, he regained much of his lost confidence and said, 'I did fall, Officer, I did, you know.'

'I'm not arguing, Kev,' I said. 'If you say you fell, then you fell, although my natural curiosity asks how you managed to get a cut of that sort just by falling. But my concern is to get you fixed, and to get it done by a doctor. There's a surgery just opposite, over there,' and I pointed to a large green door in a building with a brass plate bolted to the wall.

He said nothing as our little procession halted outside the imposing door. It was nearly twenty minutes to midnight and the whole house was in darkness. I ventured up the alley alongside, but there was no sign of a light. The doctor was in bed.

The bell-pull was one of those old-fashioned knobs with a cable attached and I hauled on this to produce a loud ringing sound within the huge house. I rang several times to produce what I hoped to be an indication of urgency, and in the mean-time looked at the pale Kev beside me.

'Release the pressure for a few seconds,' I advised him. 'We don't want to cut off your whole arm's supply of blood. The handkerchief will stop it spurting.'

He smiled briefly and nodded.

'Maybe he's away,' said Sandra.

'I hope not!' I murmured, hauling once again on the strong bell-pull. This produced lights. I rang the bell again to confirm my message of urgency, as behind me the first rush of dancers began to leave the hall. Suddenly, the market place was full of laughing, chattering people, getting into cars and hurrying home, some alone and some with their evening's conquest. I hoped the doctor didn't think the bell ringer was a late-night reveller doing it for a prank.

But more lights came on, and I could hear the deep grumbling tones of Doctor William Williams, a fiery Welshman, as he unlocked the large door.

'Pressure point on?' I smiled at Kev.

'Yeh,' he said, clinging to his arm. Sandra had an arm about his waist and I could see the shock beginning to affect him. He was starting to quiver and his face grew deathly white.

'What the hell ...' began the doctor as the huge door swung open, 'Oh, the police!'

He was dressed in a large green dressing gown and slippers, and he looked unkempt. Undoubtedly, he'd been in a deep sleep, but the sight of my uniform made him realise the bell hadn't been ringing for frivolous reasons.

'This boy is badly cut,' I said, 'He needs treatment, Doctor.'

'Does he now? Well, then, bring him into the surgery. Come in, all of you.' His musical Welsh voice sounded odd in a North Yorkshire market town, and I knew his burly, aggressive appearance concealed a warm heart.

We followed him along the passage and into the surgery where he pointed to a chair. 'Sit down,' he said to Kev. 'Now, let me see.'

Kev slowly opened his hand and Doctor Williams removed the blood-stained handkerchief. He studied the cut with care and tenderness, before saying, 'My word, a nasty one here, isn't it?'

'I'll leave now,' I offered.

'Can I stay?' asked Sandra.

'I think you'd better, girl,' smiled the doctor as he rolled up the sleeves of his dressing gown. 'Thank you, Constable, this does need treatment. Now, son,' he said, 'just let go of that muscle of yours and let's see how the blood is flowing ...'

I left them in his tender care, closed the big door behind me and resumed my patrol of the market square. Alwyn spotted me and said, 'I'll do a quick recce of the council estate. Can you look after the town centre until one o'clock?'

'Sure,' I said, breathing in the clean fresh air.

Less than five minutes later, I was walking past the side door of the King's Head Hotel when I spotted the landlord standing at the door.

He noticed me at the same instant and said, 'Oh, hello, Constable. Got a minute?'

'Of course,' and he took me into the inn, along the passage and into the gents' toilet. 'Just look at that!'

One of the small windows was broken, with a large hole apparently punched through the middle of the glass, and there was blood all over.

'I wouldn't mind if they'd come to tell me – that can't have been an accident ... nobody would be daft enough to shove a hand through there ...'

'What would it cost to replace it?' I asked him.

'Not much. Thirty bob or so.'

'If I get the villain in question to fetch the money, would that settle the matter?'

'You know who did it?'

'I've a good idea,' and I told him of the sequence of events at the dance.

'That fits what the locals said,' he confirmed. 'They said a lad with a bleeding hand rushed out of here, down the yard and out.'

'I'll see what I can do,' and I left the pub. Sure enough, the light of my torch showed a trail of blood from the yard door near the broken window, and it led the few hundred yards to the town hall, entering via the rear door.

I saw no more of the injured youth that night, but as I left the quiet market place at one o'clock that Sunday morning, the lights of Doctor Williams' surgery were still burning.

It was the following Thursday evening when I next met Kev. He was walking through Ashfordly Market

Place with Sandra on his good arm, and they spotted me standing near the monument. I was on duty, and clad in my flat cap and summer uniform, making a routine patrol of Ashfordly town centre.

The couple came towards me, with Sandra smiling broadly. She looked a picture of happiness, but Kev looked rather bashful and surprisingly shy.

'Hello.' Sandra broke the ice. 'Thanks for helping Kev last Saturday. Dr Williams was good to him, he bandaged the hand and gave him an injection.'

Kev, his pale face now showing signs of its normal colour beneath his neglected hair, looked at his arm and hand. His fist was swathed in rolls of bandage and he had his arm in a sling.

'Yeh,' he shuffled uncomfortably before me, 'Yeh, he was good. Look ...'

I waited for his speech. He was clearly not accustomed to speaking to a policeman in this way and I didn't want to dissuade him from the effort. I smiled at Sandra.

'Well,' said Kev, his feet still shuffling upon the surface of the market square, 'It's like this. I mean, no copper's ever done anything for me, not ever. Not like you did, I mean. Help. That sort of thing ...'

'It was the least I could do, Kev,' I said. 'You were hurt and it was my privilege to be able to help you. You've Sandra to thank, you know, she called me in.'

'Yeah, she's great, isn't she? Too good for me, that's true. Too good. I'm a layabout really, no bloody good to anybody. Nothing but trouble ...'

'There's good in everybody, Kev,' I said. 'Anyway, thanks for your kind words.'

'I'd like to do summat to help ... I mean ... I didn't deserve help at all ...'

'You could give the landlord of the King's Head the price of his broken window,' I suggested. 'Thirty bob.'

'You know?' he lowered his eyes in shame and stared at the ground.

'There was a trail of blood – your blood – from the window into the Town Hall. I knew that cut wasn't done in a fall – it was too clean.'

'Sorry about that, Officer. It was an accident – my mate shoved me and I fell, put my hand clean through that window, I did. Then I ran ... he did, an' all.'

'Thirty bob will square the whole thing. I want no more to do with the window – the landlord won't push for any more action if he gets the damage paid for.'

'Oh well, in that case ... I mean ... it was my fault wasn't it? For fooling about ...'

'O.K. Well, it's all over, Kev. Are you off work?'

'Yeh, till the hand's better. Look, Officer, like I said before I'm not good at saying things and I'm a right villain really, allus fighting and things ... well, I mean, I don't help the law, me nor my mates. Never. But, well, if there's trouble in any of the dances and you're needing help, well, like, I'll be there. With you, I mean. Helping you to sort 'em out. That's a promise, honest. I'll help you.'

'Thanks, Kev,' I knew what this offer must mean to him. It meant as much to me, and I made a show of attempting to shake his bandaged hand. I simply touched his right arm and wished him luck in the future.

At several of the local dances in the months that followed, I saw Kev and Sandra, and he always came across for a quiet word with me. We talked about nothing in particular, and I do know that he paid for the damaged window. But the sincerity of his promise was never tested, for I never experienced bother at any of the subsequent dances.

Nonetheless, he did attend them all, and this gave me a strong feeling of security. It still does.

Chapter 3

'No sound is dissonant which tells of life.'
SAMUEL TAYLOR COLERIDGE (1772–1834)

I AM NOT REALLY sure how I came to be a member of the Aidensfield String Orchestra. Perhaps, during some off-guard moment in a casual conversation, I let it be known that I played the violin, or it may be that some other person who knew me as a child let it be known that I could produce a tune from a battered old fiddle.

Whatever the source of the tale, I was approached by our local auctioneer, a Mr Rudolph Burley, who had heard of my doubtful prowess. He informed me there was a vacancy for a second violin in the village orchestra. I protested that I had not put bow to string for many years, and that I was as rusty as a bedspring on a council tip, but all my protestations were in vain. By the following Monday night, I was in the village hall partaking in a practice session of *Eine Kleine Nachtmusik.*

It is fair to say that the noise was awful, and that the acoustics of the hall did not help; the village piano was out of tune, and our conductor, the said Mr Burley, seemed unable to co-ordinate all sections of his 30-piece orchestra. I was never sure of the real purpose of these weekly gatherings because we attempted to play impossibly difficult pieces like Brahms' *Violin Concerto* and finished in the pub to discuss our errors. I began to wonder if it was just an excuse to visit the pub.

Because most of the practice sessions were littered with wrong notes, wrong timing, flat and sharp faults and almost every other kind of musical disgrace, the entire orchestra spent a lot of time in the pub. There were deep discussions on the best way of righting all our wrongs, and at length it was deemed the only true solution lay in two parts. The first was to comprise lots of diligent practice, and the second was to have some objective in mind, like a concert or public performance.

It was therefore decided to hold a concert in precisely one year's time. It would be in aid of village hall funds, and it is pleasing to record that this decision injected the orchestra with a new enthusiasm. Now, we had a goal; the fund for modernisation of the village hall had been stagnant for years, and had lately lacked the necessary impetus to commend it to the community. Our tuneless practice sessions, plus the publicity we began to stimulate was responsible for generating a necessary new desire to achieve something.

Fired with a fresh zeal, the rate of orchestra practice sessions was increased to two nights a week, Mondays and Thursdays. Although this put pressure on the key instrumentalists and the conductor, it did help those like myself with family commitments and duties at odd hours. Even by attending once a week, my rusty skill would be renewed.

Early that spring we started in earnest and our objective was to produce a full orchestral concert in the village hall by the following Easter.

Quite soon, the anomalous collection of people with their equally anomalous collection of instruments began to behave in a disciplined way. Our noises began to sound like real music, and I began to think that even great composers like Mozart or Chopin might have found something of interest in our enterprise. We tackled pieces like the *Violin Concerto,* but eventually decided that the concert would comprise: Mozart's *Divertimento in D*; Holst's *St Paul's Suite*; Dvorak's *Serenade*; Handel's *Concerto Grosso*; Tchaikovsky's *Serenade for Strings*; our favourite *Eine Kleine Nachtmusik*; the *Introduction and Allegro for Strings and String Quartet,* and Dag Wirren's *Serenade for Strings.*

Looking back on those halcyon days, the Aidensfield String Orchestra possessed a remarkable cross-section of the village, most of whom had delved under their beds or climbed into their attics to produce ancient violas, cellos, a double-bass, several violins and even a harp. The initial idea had come from Rudolph Burley, and it was his drive and enthusiasm that welded the group together. He could be a bully at one moment and a cajoling charmer the next, but he got results. He was a one-man committee, the sort that achieved success without the hassle of open-ended and fruitless discussions marked with opinions of great stupidity.

Rudolph was a character. He lived with a shy wife in a big house on the hill overlooking the west end of Aidensfield, and was in his late 40s. A successful auctioneer, he sold household junk by the ton, and also conducted business at cattle marts in the area, managing to make his rapid-fire voice heard above the squeak of pigs, the bellowing of bulls and the bleating of sheep. His stentorian tones were an asset when conducting the Aidensfield String Orchestra – when unwelcome sounds emanated from the music makers of the village, he could quell them with suitably loud advice.

He looked like a successful auctioneer. He had a thick mop of sandy hair which was inclined to be wavy and always untidy, and this was matched by a set of expressive eyebrows which fluctuated according to the volume of his voice. Those heavy brows lowered dramatically when he spoke softly, but when he raised his voice high enough to lift the roof of the hall, his eyebrows appeared to rise in an attempt to muffle his tones. When he was conducting, they behaved in a similar manner, rising during the crescendos and falling during the diminuendos.

His bulky figure tended to sway rhythmically during the romantic moods and jerk up and down spasmodically when things got exciting. I felt that music was bred in him even if he did stand before us in his tweed jacket, cavalry twill trousers and brogue shoes, while shouting like a salesman at a horse-market. Somehow, he coaxed sweetness from that motley collection of re-discovered musical instruments.

The double-bass player was another character of charm and fascination. His name was Ralph Hedges, and he was a retired lengthman, a man whose working life had been spent in the maintenance of our highways and byways. He was a stocky fellow with simple, grey clothing and black shoes, always clean and well kept. His rounded face was the picture of health, and he peered short-sightedly through thick spectacles during our practice sessions; turned 70, he was dependable in that he came every practice night, and he knew most of the pieces by heart. This could be a problem at times because he played them at his own speed, but Rudolph gradually tamed him.

His double-bass was ancient but its tone was mellow and beautiful and he could pluck its thick strings in a way that showed remarkable empathy between man and instrument. His strong fingers, hardened by years of working with a pick and shovel, coped easily with the powerful strings of the bass and possessed an agility that was remarkable in a man of this age. Everyone loved old Ralph.

Lovable though he was, Ralph had one very distressing habit. By this, I mean it was distressing to other, more sensitive members of the orchestra. Try as they might, they never did grow accustomed to it, for it was a habit which meant he had to be placed at the rear of the orchestra, nicely beyond the sight of any audience, and well away from those who were distracted by his noisy effusions.

The problem was that he spat on the floor as he coaxed such lovely music from his double-bass. Furthermore, he did this in time to the music, the result being that, to the count of four, the orchestra would be complemented by the sound of Ralph's spittle positively smacking upon the polished wooden floor. At times, when the pace increased, or when it was a particularly exciting piece of music, Ralph would increase his rate until he sounded like a distant herd of cows, all dropping juicy pats in time to the prevailing beat.

The snag with Ralph's problem was that if he ever dried up and failed to produce his unique, well-timed sound, there would be a vacuum in the minds of the musicians. This could cause them to miss a note, or to turn their heads away from their scores to see if the ageing Ralph was still alive. The disruption could be catastrophic during a concert.

It was suggested that the orchestra subscribed to a spittoon for him, with a never-ending supply of sawdust. The idea was rejected because, although this would save the caretaker some unpleasant work after band practice, it would not produce the particular sound of Ralph's special blend of music. He was therefore allowed to continue, and his spitting noises were accepted as a part of the orchestra's stylistic tones.

I learned that several older members were pleased to tolerate his spitting as a sign of good fortune. The custom had been practised among the ancient Greeks and Romans, and even Pliny believed it averted witchcraft. Local farmers would spit on their hands before shaking over a deal, and a large number of rural businessmen continue to spit on the first money of a deal. I think we all came to regard Ralph's musical spitting as a harbinger of good fortune for the village hall and our fund-raising efforts.

One of the orchestra's embarrassing members was the Honourable Mrs Norleigh, Rosamund to her friends. A lady of noble ancestry, so she told us, she had married plain Mr Norleigh because she loved him dearly, and the fact that he owned a chain of hotels and shops might have contributed to her romantic climb down the social scale. Embarrassing as she was, she was a valuable member of the orchestra because she played the cello with some skill, having been nurtured on the instrument in her native Surrey.

Now in her late forties, she had been rejuvenated musically and, it was rumoured, she'd also had a facial and a nose-job because of the limelight into which she was about to be thrust. She had a figure which was as exciting as a southerner's attempt at making a Yorkshire pudding and a face which did a lot for the cosmetics industry. Her noble features were rarely seen in a natural light because they were always swathed in pounds of powder and many liquid ounces of make-up. The result was something like a walking waxwork of very indeterminate age, while the clothes she wore were indicative of a lady approaching the autumn of life but who steadfastly believed she was in the eternal spring of youth.

Her most embarrassing feature was her choice of knickers. For some inexplicable reason, Rosamund always wore bright red flannelette knickers of the *directoire* type which came down to her knees, and for a cello player this was hardly the recommended dress. When she opened her legs and spread her skirts to accept the formidable breadth of the cello, she displayed yards of bright red which caused amusement or embarrassment according to the viewer's understanding of 'entertainment'.

The diplomatic Rudolph had tried positioning her to the left, to the right, in the middle row, back row and even behind the piano, but from whatever angle she was viewed, Rosamund's red knickers were visible. The only way to conceal them was to sit her facing the rear of the stage, but this was not wise because she would be unable to see the conductor. Rudolph decided the audience would have to suffer her propensity for showing off whatever she had, or for proving she'd hidden whatever she wished to hide.

The pianist, young Alan Napier, was interesting because he couldn't read a note of music. He was a farm labourer, more accustomed to milking cows and digging ditches than making music, and yet those heavy, scarred fingers could coax the most wonderful music from a piano. Even complicated pieces like concertos or major orchestral items did not deter him. For simple pieces, he would ask for them to be played through just once, and for the difficult scores, he would acquire a gramophone record.

At home, he would listen to the record and the next time he came to practise, he could play the entire piece by ear.

The lad was a born musician, but maintained he was not interested in the piano as a career; he liked to play for fun. Alan was about twenty-five years old, a single man who lived with his parents, and he had a handsome, dark face with curly black hair. Music was in him, and yet he could not sing a note, nor would he agree to being schooled in the finer art of piano-playing. He did not want his piano-playing to become a chore.

'Let me hear it, and I'll soon play it,' he would say. And he did.

This collection of country musicians, aided by a further two dozen assorted players, formed the Aidensfield String Orchestra, and there is no doubt they enjoyed their music-making. I did too; it was quite surprising how we changed from making a mess of lovely music to producing a passable piece of entertainment. It was all due to Rudolph's patience and drive.

After several months of hard but productive practice, Rudolph called for silence at one of the sessions. I was there, off duty, and was pleased to have a rest during the hard-working rehearsal.

As we paused with our instruments resting on our laps or on the floor, Rudolph wiped his brow. 'In five minutes,' he spoke gravely, 'the Colonel is going to speak to us.'

As one, we turned to look at the door behind us, but the Colonel had not arrived.

After our murmur of gentle surprise, Rudolph's loud voice quelled the speculation as he said, 'Now, I've no idea what he wants to say, but he did ask if he could address the entire orchestra tonight. He said it was a matter of importance and forthcoming pride for Aidensfield.'

More mutterings filled the room, and Rudolph halted them by emphasising some of our more noticeable weaknesses. However, he did express pleasure because our faults were fewer and our music stronger and said we were beginning to sound like a real orchestra and not something rushed together for a charity concert. We enjoyed an atmosphere of pride.

Then came the sound of the door crashing open followed by the tramp of heavy footsteps, all of which heralded the arrival of Colonel Partington and his Dalmatian. The Colonel's Christian name was Oswald and his dog was called Napoleon for reasons we never understood. Man and dog advanced into the room, and at an almost inaudible command, Napoleon sat on the floor just inside, then lay down to watch the proceedings.

The Colonel was the epitome of a retired army officer in rural Britain; stoutish in build, he bristled with belief in his own efficiency and sported a moustache which was greying like his hair. He stalked everywhere rather than walked but no one seemed quite sure where or when he had been a colonel. We assumed his friends all knew because everyone called him simply 'The Colonel'. He lived in a big house called Beckford Hall on the outskirts of Aidensfield and I suppose he occupied the unofficial position of squire to the community.

'Good evening, Colonel,' greeted Rudolph with a large smile and a loud voice.

'Good evening, Burley.' The Colonel called everyone by surname. 'A nice turn-out, what?'

'We've maintained an excellent attendance record,' beamed Rudolph like an RSM on parade. 'I'm proud of our members.'

'And their music, what? How's that coming along?'

'First class. We've mastered *Concerto Grosso* and by the date of our concert, we'll have studied and conquered enough music for a two-hour programme.'

'Good. Well, that's why I'm here. To talk to them all, what? I believe in telling everyone, not keeping things hushed up, you know.'

We waited for his news.

'Burley, you said you had planned a concert for the spring?'

'Yes, Colonel.'

'Any chance of making it a firm date, what? Say Saturday the fifteenth of April?'

'Fifteenth April?' Rudolph looked at us all for guidance, but the date meant nothing to anyone. I carried a pocket diary and checked the date – I had no private engagements that day, but it was too far in advance to know whether I'd be committed on duty.

'I'm free, subject to the exigencies of the service,' I spoke in a formal manner.

'Thank you, Rhea,' beamed the Colonel. 'What about you others, eh?'

There was some discussion among them, and it seemed that any date was suitable. There were no particular objections to a performance on Saturday 15 April, and we had time to rehearse fully before then.

'So can we make it a firm date, what?' he asked, addressing his proposal to Rudolph. I could see that Rudolph was somewhat reticent about committing himself to a date without knowing the reason, but the Colonel's status in the community did carry a certain persuasion.

Because no one made a formal objection, Rudolph

Burley agreed.

'That is marvellous,' beamed the Colonel. 'Now I can confirm it with No. 10.'

At first, no one reacted to his reference to No. 10, and I must admit the phrase did not alert me in any way. In the moment's silence that followed, Rudolph took the initiative.

'No. 10?' he asked the Colonel.

'Downing Street,' he smiled. 'The Prime Minister is my house-guest that weekend, and I thought it would be nice to fetch him to the concert. Perhaps we should officially open the renovated hall the same evening? I'll ask him to do the honours, what? And we can entertain him with a salad supper or something, and music from this orchestra. How about that?'

'The Prime Minister?' cried Rudolph.

In the excitement, Ralph spat twice in rapid succession and Rosamund's red knickers flashed as she wondered what to do with her cello. I was aghast – for me, there would be no music that night. I'd be up to the neck with security worries, and there'd be the Chief Constable, the hierarchy from the County Council, Special Branch officers, C.I.D. and a veritable entourage of officials and social climbers to cater for. I wondered if Rudolph realised the work, worry and problems he'd created by his acceptance of the Colonel's suggestion.

But he had agreed and that was that. The orchestra was so excited that everyone raised a cheer and the dog barked in happiness.

'Marvellous for the village, what?' beamed the Colonel. 'We can put on a good show for him, can't we?'

News that Aidensfield String Orchestra was going to play for the Prime Minister flashed around the village, and I thought I'd better tell Sergeant Blaketon about it. The very next day I motorcycled into Ashfordly to discuss it with him.

I located him in his office where he was working hard on a report for the Superintendent. He bore my interruption with dignity.

'Yes, Rhea? What is it?'

'A visit by the Prime Minister to Aidensfield, Sergeant,' I said, hoping to surprise him.

'Ah, yes, he's friendly with Colonel Partington. When's he coming?'

I told him, and explained about the village hall and its modernisation scheme, following with the orchestra's role in the occasion. Having satisfactorily explained all this, I then mentioned my part in the orchestra's violins.

'No chance, Rhea. On that day, you'll be officiating, on duty, in uniform, on behalf of the North Riding Constabulary. There'll be no fiddling time off that day, Rhea,' and he chuckled at his own joke.

'Thanks, Sergeant,' I smiled ruefully, knowing deep down that this must be the only course of action. 'What about the administrative arrangements for the Force during the visit?'

'I'll have words with the Superintendent. No doubt we'll be given official notification of the visit, and that will set the administrative wheels in action. On a visit of this kind, there are all kinds of official papers to worry about. But none of that's your concern, Rhea. Just be available on the day, that's all, for police duty.'

And so it was deemed that I would not play my violin for the Prime Minister and I was sure he wouldn't notice my absence. Whether he would have appreciated my skilful A flats and pizzicato expertise is something I will never know, so my only way of proving myself worthy to stand in his gaze was to make a good job of policing Aidensfield on the big day.

Even though I was not going to play before the Prime Minister, I continued with rehearsals and found it stimulating. I was privy to the arrangements on the police side, seeing them intensify as time progressed, and I was also aware of the band's internal problems. In many ways, I was the liaison officer between the orchestra and the police, and found myself advising on the best position for the conductor to stand, the route to be taken from Colonel Partington's home to the hall and sundry other practical details.

As time went by, the event gained in stature. The occasion started to acquire people who wanted to be part of the accepted guest list. Before we realised what had happened, the vicar had persuaded the Archbishop of York to say a few words prior to the concert, then the local parish council, district council and county council all felt they should be represented, and so did a party of obscure gentlemen who reckoned they'd belonged to the Colonel's old Regiment. The British Legion, Women's Institute, Parochial Church Council, Meals on Wheels, Black-faced Sheepbreeders' Association, Catholic Women's League, Ryedale Historical Society, Ashfordly Literary and Philosophical Society, the League of Rural Artists, Country Landowners' Association, the Labour Party, and sundry other organisations all wanted to be part of the act. The poor Colonel had the devil's own job fitting everyone in because all the officials reckoned they deserved seats with their names on, all at the front, and all next to the Prime Minister.

The poor people of Aidensfield found themselves being thrust further and further into the background as fewer and fewer seats became available for them – in their own village hall. There were the inevitable complaints and grumbles, but as the official wheels began to turn inexorably, there was nothing any of them could do. Officialdom, plus its tail of petty politics, had, in all its horror, came to Aidensfield, and it was the last thing anyone wanted or needed.

Like everyone else, I was acutely aware of the upset this had caused, and I knew there was nothing anyone could do about it. Or was there? Officialdom, once it takes over, does not cater for the wishes of the real people; it caters for society types in high positions and minor politicians, and because the PM himself was to grace our hall with his presence, every petty official for miles around began to wheedle his or her way on to the guest list.

I'm sure the PM would not have wished this to happen; I'm sure that when Colonel Partington honoured us by suggesting the great man visited our concert, he visualised the PM taking a seat like anyone else in the village, without any formalities and fuss.

But it didn't work out like that. The chairman of the parish council had to make a formal speech of welcome, following which the Archbishop would make an address, and then countless other minor officials and local politicians wanted to say their piece. All this was written down in an official programme, and even if everyone took only two minutes over their individual speeches, the programme would be prolonged by nearly forty minutes.

The affair was out of hand. I had no doubt about that, and when I received my formal copy of the approved programme, I saw that the final speech, before the concert started, was a *second* address by the Archbishop of York who would say the Lord's Prayer. As the 'Amen' sounded from the assembled mass of officials and few villagers, my job was to raise the curtain on stage and signal the band to commence with our beautifully rehearsed *Introduction and Allegro for Strings*.

My task on stage, albeit behind the scenes, was allocated to me for several reasons. First, there was the question of security on stage during the concert, and I could keep an eye on the rear entrance; secondly, I was familiar with the orchestral pieces and could maintain a liaison between the orchestra and the Colonel, who in turn would inform the PM if there was a break for him to 'retire' as it is nicely phrased; and thirdly, I was to act as liaison between the audience, the official programme, and the conductor. My role was therefore of considerable importance.

My most important duty of the night however, was personally to raise the curtain as the Archbishop said his final 'Amen' after all the speeches, the signal to start the concert. I was to alert Rudolph seconds before doing so, so that he could prepare the orchestra: as the curtain rose, the hall would be filled with the music of the Aidensfield String Orchestra.

The final days passed in a blur of activity, and the hall looked resplendent in its coat of new paint, fresh curtains, polished woodwork, scrubbed floor, carpets in strategic places and flowers inside and out. Half an hour before the PM was due to take his seat, the place was packed and from my vantage point on stage behind the curtain, I could see the rows of petty officials who had wormed their way into this place, to deprive many villagers of their moment of pride and pleasure.

Rudolph knew of my anger. He felt the same. Together, we peered through a gap in the curtain as the hall buzzed with anticipation.

'I'd like to kick that lot out!' he said vehemently. 'Look at them – sitting there in their posh hats and new suits, just because it's the Prime Minister ... this was a village concert, Nick, not a bloody excuse for ingratiating themselves with him ...'

As we stared at them, an awful scheme entered my mind. At first, I tried to dislodge the notion, but the more I tried, the more feasible it seemed.

'We could cut out all those speeches, Rudolph,' I said quietly.

'Could we?' Even his loud whisper almost deafened me at this range. 'They're all in the bloody programme! We can't cut them out ...'

'If I cut half an hour off those introductory speeches, can you fill it with music before the finale?'

He grinned wickedly.

'We can. We've rehearsed enough for three concerts.'

'Right,' I said. 'I'll take responsibility for this. I'll have an accident ... can your members all be on stage and ready to go by the time the Archbishop has finished his *first* speech? Not the prayers?'

'Just leave it to me!' and off he went.

At seven-thirty, everyone was in position. The hall was full, and prompt on the stroke of the half-hour, the Prime Minister, to polite applause, entered Aidensfield Village Hall and took his seat. I was behind the curtains, with my hand on the handle which would raise them at the right moment, and I was peeping through the gap, watching the proceedings in the hall. On stage, Rudolph and the orchestra were ready. He was poised in his evening suit, baton at the ready, and he had warned the players about their earlier than scheduled performance.

I waited as the chairman of the parish council, the chief citizen of Aidensfield, officially welcomed our distinguished guest. This was an important part of the ceremony, and he spoke well. The Archbishop climbed on to the steps before the stage and welcomed the PM, as Head of Her Majesty's Government, to the Diocese of York. Having made his speech, he prepared to dismount, and his place was to be taken by the first of a long line of mini-officials, all with boring words to say.

This was my moment.

I raised my hand.

Rudolph saw it; he brought his orchestra to a state of readiness, and before the next speaker could reach the foot of the steps, I pressed the lever and the curtain rose. There was a long pause before the hall erupted into an explosion of applause, and Rudolph was already bringing the orchestra into the first notes of the *Introduction and Allegro.*

From my place behind the scenes, I saw the looks of apprehension and disappointment from the assembled minor officials, the smiles of glee on the villagers seated behind, a look of pleasurable anticipation on the Prime Minister's face, and happy smiles by all players in the orchestra. Old Ralph was spitting bang on time, and Rosamund's knickers were in full view of the Prime Minister, so tonight she wore blue ones.

Afterwards, when it was all over and he'd opened the refurbished village hall, the Prime Minister came backstage to thank us all. Rudolph introduced me as the man whose duty it was to raise the curtains at the start, and who was in charge of security backstage.

The Prime Minister looked at me quizzically, asked if I'd had any security problems, and then said? 'You got us off to a flying start, P.C. Rhea. Well done.'

But I still had to face the Superintendent and Sergeant Blaketon.

Colonel Partington accompanied the Superintendent as he followed in the official party and when he reached me, the Colonel said, 'Rhea, the PM says you did a good job tonight, getting us off to such a flying start. He's asked you to take sherry with us at my home tomorrow before lunch. Do join us, Rhea.'

'It will be a pleasure, sir,' I smiled, and the Superintendent said nothing, therefore Sergeant Blaketon maintained his silence.

Chapter 4

'Life itself is but the shadow of death.'
SIR THOMAS BROWNE (1605–82)

VERY FURTIVELY, AND WITH utter contempt for rules and regulations, Patrick Hughes set about establishing a caravan site on a patch of scrub land at the extremities of his ranging farm near Elsinby.

Being an astute businessman, who saw money in this useless earth, Patrick recognised the potential profits to be made from tourism, albeit on a minor scale, and so he purchased half a dozen second-hand caravans. Using his Land-Rover, he towed these shabby vehicles one by one from their point of purchase, and installed them on his lumpy piece of unprofitable land, known locally as Alder Carrs.

To be fair to Patrick, the land in question had no possible use in agriculture because it was very rocky in places and riddled with deep hollows full of marshes and reeds. It could never be ploughed or cultivated. It simply existed on the outer edge of his farm, well away from the village and hidden from the road. The caravan-site idea was typical of Patrick's desire to earn money from every square inch of his land.

He positioned his six caravans around Alder Carrs so that each had an extensive view across Upper Ryedale, and it must be said that he worked hard to make this new enterprise a success. He wanted his visitors to have as many home comforts as he could muster and he saw his site as the Mecca for a new breed of discerning caravanners.

He painted all the vans in a pleasing shade of tan so that they merged with the surrounding countryside, and gave each the name of a flower – a charming idea, I felt. Thus we had Primrose, Bluebell, Buttercup, Daisy, Violet and Snowdrop and I did wonder if this was to baffle any tax man who might inspect his accounts, because these were typical of the names given to cows.

No one seemed to question his choice of nomenclature, and having beautified his vehicles by painting a picture of the appropriate bloom upon each one, he built a small area with a rubble base for a car park. Next, he installed rubble paths to all the vans, and even erected a double-seater flush toilet in a secluded place, with a small shelter adjoining the latter sporting two cold taps and a drain. Waste and sewage from Alder Carrs Wash Room, as he called it, and from the toilets of both the caravan site and the farm itself (i.e. the house and outbuildings), flowed down the hillside in pipes to a sewage pit which had been a feature of the farm for many years.

The pit was necessarily a long way from the village and from Patrick's domestic quarters because the merest hint of warm weather made it somewhat mephitic. When the wind was in the wrong direction on a hot day, Elsinby's patient villagers would get a whiff of the effluvium but as it was not much stronger than Patrick's muckspreading activities, no one complained. Agricultural fumes of varying potency are generally accepted as part of rural life, and so the sewage pit remained to satisfy the needs of Alder Farm and the local fly population.

It was a deep pit, very sensibly positioned, and it had been adequately fenced right from the moment of its construction; that fence was inspected by Patrick before his first intake of campers and he decided that it was adequate to deter children and adults from running headlong into his pit of feculence. He reasoned, in a typical countryman's way, that if any children or adults were daft enough to climb over the fence, the very smell and appearance of the place would deter them from venturing further.

Having established his site in what he considered a very professional manner, Patrick set about attracting some visitors. He advertised in papers local to the big cities and called his site The Garden of Ryedale. The little paths about the site were called Leafy Ways, the shed with the cold water tap was Water Lily House, the car park was Forget-me-Not (because he hoped people would never leave their vehicles unlocked – a nice touch, I felt), while the toilet block was appropriately named Meadow Sweet.

Milk, eggs and vegetables could be purchased from Patrick's wife at the farmhouse and he agreed to let them use the telephone upon payment. In all, it was a worthy enterprise, its only failing being that it did not have the blessing of the appropriate authorities such as the Rural District Council. They did not know it existed and Patrick felt that application for permission was a waste of time because it might be refused.

Like the Council, I knew nothing of the Garden of Ryedale until I received a telephone call just after eight-thirty one Wednesday morning in June.

'P.C. Rhea,' I announced.

'Is that the policeman?' came the distant voice of a

man who sounded worried.

'Yes,' I acknowledged.

'And is Elsinby under you?' the voice continued.

'Yes, it is on my beat. Can I help you?'

'Well, it's my son and his wife. They're in a caravan at The Garden of Ryedale Caravan Site and I want a message getting to them. I don't know the name of the proprietor. I wondered if you could possibly deliver it for me – it's urgent and it's family.'

The delivery of such messages was a regular feature of my work as a rural policeman, especially when so many isolated homes did not have a telephone. It was a worthwhile service because it brought me into close contact with the people in a helpful way. This particular call was destined to bring me into very close contact with the Garden of Ryedale Caravan Site and Patrick's smelly sewage pit.

My caller was a Mr J. C. Hicks, and his son was called Alan. Alan and his young wife, Jennifer, were caravanning there for two weeks, and the news was that Jennifer's mother had collapsed in Birmingham. She was in hospital in a serious condition. I told Mr Hicks that I had never heard of the Garden of Ryedale Caravan Site, but in a small village like Elsinby it would not be difficult to find. I set off immediately, hoping to catch the young couple before they left on a day's outing and said I would get Jennifer to ring Mr Hicks, senior, at a number I obtained from him.

I told Mary where I was heading, and said I'd be back for lunch around twelve-thirty. I decided to spend the morning in Elsinby after carrying out this humane duty, but my first job was to find The Garden of Ryedale.

This was comparatively easy because I simply called at Elsinby Post Office and asked Gilbert Kingston, the local post-master, if he knew where I could find it.

'Aye,' he said readily. 'It's on Patrick Hughes' farm – Alder Farm, you know,' and he pointed in the general direction.

'Is it a big site?' I asked, wondering why I hadn't come across it before.

'No, only half a dozen caravans. Patrick's only just got it established, Mr Rhea. I think his first customers arrived at Easter.'

'Thanks, Gilbert.' I smiled my thanks and left his premises.

I arrived at Alder Farm less than ten minutes later, and found Patrick working in the foldyard. He was an amiable man in his mid-forties with a head of thick grey wavy hair, and several days' growth of beard on his face. His eyes were warm and brown, while his face shone with the ruddy colour of a man who spends his days in the open air. His clothing comprised a pair of heavy corduroy trousers, black wellingtons and a battered brown sweater with holes in the sleeves. On his head was a flat cap which went everywhere with him, and he had a heavy muck-fork in his hands.

As I parked my motorcycle against the wall of an outbuilding, he ceased his work and strode towards me, a big smile on his face.

'Now then, Mr Rhea, thoo's out and about early today?'

''Morning, Patrick. How's life?'

'Grand. Very pleasant, especially on a summer day like this.'

He was right. The countryside was at its best, and the warm June breezes were filled with buzzing insect life and caressing sunshine.

'Patrick, you've a caravan site they tell me?'

'Aye, it's down on Alder Carr. Nowt wrong, is there?'

'No.' I knew nothing of any rules or regulations governing the establishment of such sites, for the enforcement of such rules and regulations were not within the scope of a police officer's duty. I was ignorant of the fact that Patrick had never made formal application, and indeed, such a lapse on his part was no concern of mine.

'Oh,' he said. 'Down there then, Mr Rhea.' He pointed to a gate at the bottom of the yard and I saw the new track of rubble and gravel.

'Thanks,' and to put his mind at rest, I explained the purpose of my visit.

'Hicks? They're in Primrose,' he informed me. 'T'names are on t'doors and there's a primrose on t'van.'

'Primrose, eh?' and I decided to walk down his new road. It was very uneven, but within five minutes I was standing in the centre of his little site, looking for Primrose. I found it, and could see a young woman busy in the tiny kitchen. I approached and she noticed me; there was surprise on her face, then alarm. As I reached the door of her caravan, she had already opened it and was looking down at me with her pretty face creased in worry.

'Mrs Hicks?' I asked.

She nodded, drying her hands on a towel.

I gave her the information I'd received from her father-in-law and she asked if I knew anything more. I said I did not, but felt sure Patrick would allow her to telephone her relatives and the hospital from the farmhouse.

'My husband's gone for a walk near the river,' she

73

said. 'I'll leave a note in case he comes back while I'm at the farm.'

She had difficulty finding a pen, so I loaned her mine and waited as she scribbled the message, then accompanied her to the farmhouse. Patrick was still forking in the foldyard and readily agreed to help, so we waited together at a discreet distance as the girl made her calls. She emerged from the house looking white and anxious.

'It's my mother,' she said. 'She's been taken into hospital. I must go to her, she's critical. I'll go back to the van for my husband ...'

Patrick smiled at her. 'Look, luv,' he said kindly. 'Just leave everything here if you want to be off. If you decide not to return to finish the holiday, let me know and I'll knock summat off. You see to your mam, that's your first job.'

Smiling her thanks, she hurried back to locate her husband.

'Thoo'll have a coffee, Mr Rhea?' Patrick looked at his watch, 'It's gittin' on for 'lowance time.'

I joined him and his wife in the large kitchen of their comfortable house. Mrs Connie Hughes was a large, angular woman with a mop of black hair tied back in a rough bun, but she was kind and amiable. She produced a plate of cakes and a mug of hot, steaming coffee for us all. This kind of hospitality is enjoyed by all rural bobbies, and we chatted about life in the area, and about Patrick's new venture. Connie said she enjoyed the companionship it provided because Alder Farm was a lonely place, especially when Patrick was at market or away on business.

None of us could have known that at this precise moment, Miss Fiona Lampton was heading towards the farm on her hunter. He was a large chestnut horse called Apollo. If we had known, it would not have mattered a great deal because there was a public footpath through the bottom of Patrick's land, not far from Alder Carrs, and it was regularly used by people on foot and by horse riders. The picturesque path twisted and turned among the trees beside the river banks, and would undoubtedly be used by visitors to The Garden of Ryedale.

Fiona Lampton was a very horsey lady approaching forty summers, and she had a private income. This allowed her to indulge in her passion for keeping horses and she had several, but it had never attracted a husband for her. If her money was attractive, her horsey appearance and demeanour could be a little off-putting for anyone not closely associated with the pastime. Not even horsey men appeared to find her romantic.

Due to having considerable periods of spare time, therefore, she found herself involved in lots of village affairs at Aidensfield where she lived in a cottage, and one of her passions of the moment was conservation of the countryside. She had become involved with many groups who worked to keep the countryside free from all that would destroy it; she happened to believe that caravans were a growing menace, which explained her presence near Alder Carrs that morning. It seemed that when word of Patrick's enterprise reached her ears, she had decided to carry out her own inspection before deciding what action, if any, she should take.

And so it was that Miss Fiona Lampton aboard Apollo approached The Garden of Ryedale just as I was enjoying a coffee with Patrick and his wife. At exactly the same time, young Mrs Hicks was running about, urgently trying to trace her perambulating husband who was somewhere in the same vicinity.

The precise sequence of events is not very clear, but having talked to all the participants, I believe they occurred rather like this.

Mrs Hicks, knowing that her husband was likely to be away for another hour or so, resorted to a device they'd employed while camping in tents. If one of them wished to attract the attention of the other, while away, they would seize the frying pan in one hand, and a large tablespoon in the other. By thumping the bottom of the frying pan with the spoon, considerable noise can be generated, and this can be reinforced by persistent shouting. Young Mrs Hicks therefore decided to adopt this husband-tracing technique by standing on the top of one of Patrick's rocky outcrops on Alder Carrs, and clouting the frying pan for all it was worth. She reasoned that the sound would carry to all corners of this peaceful glade.

There is no doubt it seemed a good idea at the time, particularly as the din *did* reach the ears of the wandering Mr Hicks. He recognised the urgency of his wife's summons, and at the time, had been standing on a high boulder in the wood, stretching his neck to inspect a nuthatch's nest high in a dead tree. Upon hearing the significant tones of the frying pan, followed by his wife's call, he had leapt off the boulder, crashed through the broken twigs and rubbish, and then galloped out of the trees towards the woodland path.

In so doing, his movements were rather noisy; it was somewhat akin to an elephant dashing through the jungle, and he was shouting too. The noise startled Miss Fiona's nervous mount. She had difficulty controlling Apollo during those hectic moments, and he almost got away from her; he jumped and bucked with alarm at the crashing noises and raucous human voice which came out of the trees, but managed to work his nervous way along the path. Fiona had him under control, a tribute to her skill.

But just as Miss Fiona had calmed the anxious beast, horse and rider turned a bend and there, in full view, was Alder Carrs; at that moment, the horse saw Mrs Hicks standing aloft on a pinnacle of granite and belabouring the frying pan for all she was worth. She was shouting too, and behind was the crashing in the wood. These curious noises and waving arms were all too much for the nervous Apollo.

He bolted. Ears laid back in terror, he opened his powerful legs and moved across the land as if his heels had wings. Aboard, Miss Fiona shouted, kicked and hauled on the reins but Apollo was having none of it. He wanted to be free from these weird noises and sights and no amount of horsemanship would persuade him to remain.

Unfortunately, his flight path led towards the tidy fence which surrounded Patrick's sewage pit.

Rather as one would expect from Pegasus, the legendary winged horse, Apollo soared over the fence quite heedless of the pervading smells. Just as Pegasus had kicked Mount Helicon to create the fountain of the Muses, so Apollo kicked the surface of the stinking pond to create a fountain of the messes. But unlike Pegasus, Apollo was not able to fly across the waters. He landed in the middle with Miss Fiona still on board and he immediately sank amid a colossal spray of foul-smelling effluent.

When the evil spray settled like the canopy of a parachute, it enveloped both horse and rider as they sank into the horrible depths; Apollo began to fight for his survival, while Miss Fiona clung to his neck because there was nothing else to cling to and besides, she couldn't see anything due to the coating of slime which bathed her face. She lay along his broad back and shouted, as he fought to climb out of the slurry.

But the more he fought, the more he sank, and the more he sank the more he fought. The slippery ooze threatened to remove Miss Fiona's grip and its thick texture prevented Apollo from swimming through it. It was too fluid to provide any kind of platform and he sank until his feet touched the bottom. Only his head and neck showed, with Miss Fiona clinging to these life-saving parts of him. Gradually, he became very still; exhaustion caused him to give up the battle and he sensibly allowed things to settle about him.

Miss Fiona dared not dismount; she could never swim through this mess and if she dismounted, she would sink over her head anyway. So she sat as still as a mouse, waiting. She wiped her eyes, her aquiline nose twitching at the awful stench that assailed her, and she began to shout for help.

Fortunately, the couple who were the cause of Apollo's sudden gallop were on hand to witness his sticky end, and they quickly sized up the situation. Mr Hicks shouted for Fiona to sit still and said he'd call for help.

That's how I became involved.

Leaving the Hicks couple to rush off to Birmingham, Patrick rang the Fire Brigade and explained the situation, then we both went down to the sewage pit to see what could be done. There was nothing we could do, but the flies were having a super time, dive bombing and tasting the delicacies so fortuitously presented to them.

'She'll etti sit tight, Mr Rhea,' advised Patrick. 'If she tumbles inti that crap, she'll vanish for ivver.' Then he shouted, 'Hold on, Miss Fiona. Sit tight. That awd gallower o' thine'll sit tight if thoo lets him …'

And so we waited for the Fire Brigade.

The Fire Brigade, with the expertise of its members for coping with peculiar situations, is beyond compare and it seems that our local brigade were quite accustomed to rescuing cows which got into this sort of difficulty. When they arrived, it was a remark by Patrick that reminded me of this skill, when he said, 'Thoo'll be used ti gitting coos oot o' spots like that?' His use of words did cause me to wonder about his opinion of Miss Fiona, however.

The Fire Brigade team used equipment they had brought, and, with the grateful help of Miss Fiona, they attached a harness to Apollo, with a sling around his rump, and simply hauled him from the mess. He emerged with a hollow sucking noise, kicked his legs in delight, and whinnied his happiness. Fiona slid off him with a squelching sound, thanked the firemen from a safe distance, then mounted Apollo to ride home. She was accompanied by cheers from the gathered assembly, which now included some caravanners, and a fair selection of flies and assorted muck-living insects which escorted her home in the form of a happy cloud.

'Thoo'll have a cup of coffee, you fellers?' suggested Patrick, and the firemen accepted. After swilling off the muck, they drank their coffee in his farmyard, and the senior man present said, 'We'll have to make our usual report about this.'

The significance of that remark escaped both Patrick and me, but three weeks later it resulted in the Public Health Inspector visiting the farm to inspect this hitherto unknown caravan site. And he promptly closed it down until the sewage disposal arrangements were made satisfactory.

As Patrick later said of Miss Fiona, 'That bloody woman's gitten a drastic way of doing things.'

I had to agree.

It was George Eliot in *Mr Gilfil's Love Story* who said, 'Animals are such agreeable friends,' and this was personified in the partnership of Mr Aaron Harland and his dog, Pip.

Aaron was a retired quarryman, a widower who lived alone in a terrace cottage at Thackerston. He kept the place as clean as the proverbial new pin, and in his retirement went upon long walks around the countryside. He was a friendly man, very quiet and thoughtful, and his round, clean face bore thick spectacles which always needed cleaning. I often wondered if he thought his home was covered in dust; he spent his life peering through it, and it occurred to me that this was probably the outcome of a life-time's work in the dust of quarrying. Perhaps he thought the world was in a dust cloud.

His dog, Pip, was a Jack Russell terrier, a small pert dog with a short tail and two black ears. Its coat was tough and wiry, and it stood little more than a foot in height.

Man and dog went everywhere together. The little terrier was never restricted by a leash, and spent its time investigating rabbit warrens, hedge backs, holes in barn walls and other places where rats, mice and possible prey might lurk. And if creatures did hide there, Pip would flush them out and enjoy a rapid scamper across the countryside in pursuit.

Jack Russell terriers are essentially working dogs, and they are good at ratting which makes them popular with countrymen. They're also an asset in fox-hunting because they will enter the fox's earth and will bark when they discover the whereabouts of Reynard. These quick, lively little dogs love to work and revel in exercise, but they are small enough to be a companionable house pet as well. There is little wonder many countrymen keep them.

I would often meet Aaron and Pip as they went on their perambulations around Thackerston, and we always stopped for a chat. Sometimes, if Aaron was working in his tiny garden, or was on his way home from the post office, he would invite me into the house for a cup of tea and a chat, a pleasant diversion for me. On the occasions I did pop in, Pip would sniff suspiciously at my legs, look me over once or twice, and then settle down on an old rug which Aaron placed near the fireside. His short tail would pump with happiness for a few seconds before his bright, alert eyes closed in what appeared to be a nap.

Aaron would invariably tell me about the quarry where he'd worked for most of his life, digging out limestone by the ton, and he would tell me all about the district too. When his wife died over twenty years ago, Aaron took to studying the history of the district and became quite an authority, but he never wrote it down.

There were many times during our fireside talks when I pleaded with him to write down his memories and findings, but he never did. One day, I hope he will – the last time I saw him, he was approaching eighty and was still talking of his researches, still discovering more of Thackerston's past and still keeping a Jack Russell terrier for companionship.

Pip died some years ago, but it was his adventurous spirit that caused an upset one April.

Aaron and Pip had embarked on one of their long

walks, and because the April sun was bringing the countryside to life, they walked a little further and a little longer than usual. Aaron had, in fact, walked to his former place of work, Thackerston Quarry, which lay well over a mile from the village.

It was now disused; the floor was full of discarded rubble and abandoned machinery. There was rusting metalwork everywhere, yards of miniature railway lines, old trucks, winding gear, diesel engines and a host of forgotten equipment. Where men had once scraped a living from the steep sides of stone, there now flourished willow herbs, wild briars and a multitude of rock plants, while large pools of dusty water stood in hollows about the quarry floor. An old hut, battered by the weather, occupied a corner site and there was a tiny brick-built office near the entrance, with a table and chair inside. On the table was a dirty old teapot and three mugs, relics of someone's last tea-break.

In Aaron's day, this place had been a hive of activity, with teams of wagons coming to cart away the work of the day, and the quarry had played a social role in the village. The workers and their families had become a close community, while the owner of the quarry had looked after them as best he could. He had provided aid for housing them, occasionally giving them a bonus based on the profits earned and striving to keep them in work by finding more outlets for his quarried material. Aaron had retired from the quarry and now lived on his savings and a pension, but soon after he'd left, the quarry had closed. Now, it was like a deserted wild-west scenario, a haven for animals and plants where the sound of insects had replaced the rumble of busy machines.

For Aaron, that return to the quarry must have produced happy memories; he must have heard again the voices of his former colleagues and friends, the noise of the machinery and the crumple of explosives as new paths were made into the solid walls of the quarry. He must have experienced anew the unmistakable scents of the place, the chatter of the men, the hooter telling them it was break time, the constant presence of rising dust …

For Pip, on the other hand, the quarry was a haven of different delights. There were fascinating holes to explore, animals to hunt, smells to investigate and things to cock his leg against. Pip scurried around the quarry in a frenzy of canine activity, uncertain which of his many options to follow.

As Aaron shuffled about the floor, kicking old buckets, handling old equipment and thinking of old friends, Pip darted into a crevice in hot pursuit of anything that might live there. There could be rabbits, rats, foxes, mice, almost any living creature. In he went, tail wagging, on what for him was an exploration of delight.

But he never came out.

For about half an hour after Pip's entry, Aaron continued his journey into nostalgia, completely oblivious of his little friend's exploration. Finally, having wallowed in his memories to a state of satisfaction, he looked at his watch and decided it was time to go home for tea.

'Pip?' he called as he always did, expecting the game little dog to bark its response.

But there was no response.

'Pip?'

Poor Aaron stumbled about the uneven floor of the quarry calling for his dog, but Pip never came. We will never know what passed through Aaron's mind during those awful minutes, but I do know that he went home to see if Pip had returned for any reason. There being no Pip at the house, he returned to the quarry to see if he was there. Many times, he did this and each time the outcome was the same. There was no Pip at either place to bark a welcome and wag that stumpy tail.

With all his quarrying experience, and with his knowledge of Jack Russell terriers, Aaron feared the worst. Pip must have entered one of the countless crevices in the limestone, and was now trapped underground. It had happened many times before with dogs; dogs hunting foxes had become trapped or lost in endless burrows and some had never been seen again. Old quarries were always a source of trouble for inquisitive dogs, and there is nothing more inquisitive than a hunting Jack Russell ...

Bravely, Aaron kept his awful secret until next morning. He spent an overnight vigil in the quarry, repeatedly calling for Pip and shouting his name into all the crevices and cracks, hoping against hope for that single distinctive bark in response. Jack Russells did bark when they found anything, and this one barked at the sound of its own name.

Why on earth Aaron failed to tell anyone we shall never know but I reckon it was his Yorkshire canniness coupled with a belief that he could solve his own problems. I should imagine that he didn't want to be embarrassed in his sorrow and that he did not want to put others to any trouble on his behalf. For all those reasons and more Aaron Harland kept his lonely vigil during that April night.

Next morning, I was on early patrol, starting at six o'clock on my Francis Barnett to tour the outlying villages and communities. These early tours were a regular part of my work – we performed one late and one early each week, and they were a way of showing our presence at unusual hours.

On this occasion, my first port of call was the telephone kiosk in Thackerston where I had to make a point at 6.40 a.m. While travelling down the gently sloping incline into the village, I noticed the weary figure of Aaron trudging homewards. There was something not right about him, and for a moment, I couldn't decide what it was.

I pulled up ahead of him, and sat astride the machine until he reached me. He looked terrible. His face was ashen and unshaven, and his feet and hands were covered in limestone grime and mud. His hair and clothing were dusty too, and he was almost exhausted.

'Aaron!' I must have sounded alarmed. 'What's the matter?'

He shook his old head and I could see the beginnings of tears in his eyes; then I realised what was not right about him. Pip was not by his side.

'It's Pip,' he said. 'He's gone.'

'Gone?' At this stage I had no idea how or where he'd gone.

'Up in t'quarry,' he mumbled sorrowfully.

'Has he fallen over the cliff?' I asked, struggling to get the full story from him.

He shook his head. 'Nay, lad, I think he's gone into the quarry face, up on one o' them fissures. Jack Russells do that, go into spots seeking foxes and rabbits.'

'When?' I asked, and he told his story, explaining how he'd searched everywhere outside the quarry too, and how he knew, in his heart of hearts, that Pip had got lost in the labyrinth of cracks underground. He told me about the qualities of limestone, and how it lent itself to long fissures which could stretch for miles beneath the surface of the earth, sometimes opening up as colossal caves or underground lakes. No one knew what lay deep behind that disused quarry face.

'Won't he find his own way out?' I asked.

'He might,' Aaron shrugged his shoulders. 'Nobody can tell.'

'Is there anything I can do?' I asked, relying on his experience as an ex-quarryman.

'Nay, lad, there's nowt. I'll just etti wait and see.'

'How long can he last without food?' I put to the old man.

'It's hard to say.' He was honest. 'Four, five days mebbe, even longer. He might have found summat under there, mind. Rabbits, mice and things, and water. He'll need water, Mr Rhea.'

'So if he's not injured, he could live for a long time in there and come out safely?'

'Aye, he could,' and his final word was filled with uncertainty.

I knew that Aaron wanted his little friend to be found safe and well, and there seemed so little anyone could do for him. The agony was in the waiting, and the waiting was full of imponderables.

'Jump on the pillion,' I said. 'I'll take you home.'

Aaron obeyed, clambering stiffly on to my motorcycle, and I carried him the final half-mile to his little house.

'I've got a point to make, Aaron, but I'll be back in ten minutes. You get yourself some breakfast, then we'll talk about it.'

I watched him enter his house, a shade of his normal, happy self, and felt that something should be done for him. But what could be done? How could anyone help? As luck would have it, Sergeant Bairstow made one of his rare visits to me at my 6.40 a.m. point and asked, 'Anything doing, Nick?'

I told him about Aaron and his missing dog, and Sergeant Bairstow said, 'Poor old bugger! Has he been out all night?'

I explained the full situation, and Sergeant Bairstow agreed with me. Something must be done and he believed he had the answer. He said he would meet me at my 7.10 a.m. point which was in Ploatby, but in the meantime, he advised me not to build up the old man's hopes. It was necessary to fear the worst.

While I went for a cup of tea with Aaron, Sergeant Bairstow drove away in the official car upon his mystery mission; I asked Aaron not to go traipsing around the countryside searching for Pip, and promised I would visit the quarry regularly this morning to see if he had emerged. Aaron appeared content with this – at least, his problem was now shared, but I did not tell him about the sergeant's discussion.

Twenty-five minutes later, I drove across to Ploatby and waited outside that telephone kiosk at the appointed time, and sure enough, Sergeant Bairstow turned up. He was smiling.

'Great news, Nick,' he greeted me as he stepped out of the vehicle. 'Today, we're going to attempt the rescue of that dog.'

'Are we?' I asked. 'How, exactly?'

'Jim Fairburn, to be precise. He owns Chaffleton Quarry. You know it?'

'Yes, I do.' It was a large, busy concern just off the road to Malton.

'Nice chap, is Jim,' Sergeant Bairstow said, 'and he owes me a big favour. I've told him about the dog and he's sending his men up to Thackerston this morning to blow that old quarry to pieces.'

'What about the dog?' I cried.

'He'll cope with that, he's not daft,' said Charlie Bairstow with confidence. 'The explosions will clean the face away, but leave the underground intact, so he says. It's all done by experts. He owns Thackerston Quarry, by the way; he bought it when it became exhausted, and says he's been thinking about examining the limestone to see if it is workable. Today will serve two purposes – hopefully, we'll find that dog, and he'll have an excuse for working the old quarry to see if it is viable. It could do us all some good.'

'What about Aaron?' I asked. 'Should he be there to see it?'

'That's a tricky one. What do you think?'

I tried to put myself into Aaron's shoes. It wasn't easy. All I could say was, 'I reckon he'd want to be there. If we did find Pip, or if the dog got killed in the work that's going on, I'm sure he'd want to know.'

'O.K. Go back and tell him. They'll start about half past eight, after Jim's ferried the men and the equipment up from Chaffleton. If Aaron wants to watch, he can, but he'll have to do as he's told by the foreman.'

'He's been doing that all his life.' I smiled, and then I remembered something else about Aaron. I caught Sergeant Bairstow in time.

'Sergeant!' I called after him. 'Forget what we said about Aaron witnessing the rescue. We'd better not tell him it's a rescue attempt, and then he won't be disappointed if it fails. Besides, he's an independent old cuss and would hate to think *he* didn't find Pip.'

'Fair enough, so what do we tell him?'

'Just that Jim Fairburn is doing some exploratory work in Thackerston Quarry today; we'll say he's been told about the dog, but his real reason is to examine the old quarry to see if it is workable.'

'Good idea. I'll brief Jim about that and you can tell Aaron. If Aaron wants to come along, then that'll be fine. Let's hope it works, Nick.'

And so the plot was prepared. I returned to Aaron's house after making a second point at 8.10 a.m. at Thackerston telephone kiosk, and gave him the news. He looked at me through those dusty spectacles, and said, 'If they kill my dog with their new-fangled quarrying, I'll nivver forgive 'em. These new fellers aren't quarrymen, they're explosives experts, nowt else. They know nowt about quarrying, none of 'em. Aye, Mr Rhea, I'll go and see they keep my dog from getting blown to bits. I'll keep an eye on 'em.'

I conveyed him there, complete with some sandwiches and a flask of coffee, so he could spend the day observing events in Thackerston Quarry.

I did not stay because I had other duties to occupy me, although I did pop in from time to time. The place was a hive of activity with lorries, a crane, mechanical diggers, JCBs and a host of other heavy and light equipment. Dust was flying and I realised why Aaron's glasses were always dirty – it was a state of normality for him. Already, heaps of fallen rock lay about and men were busy on the cliff face. Every fifteen minutes or so there was an explosion as more rock was blown into small fragments, and I could see the anxious figure of Aaron hovering on the periphery of the work.

I found Jim Fairburn and asked, 'Any luck?'

He shook his head sadly. 'Nothing. Not a sign, and not a whimper. I reckon his dog's gone miles underground, Mr Rhea; it might take days to come back here, if it ever makes it.'

'It's good of you to do this for him.'

'Think nothing of it. It was a job we had to do anyway, and we can use the stuff we've moved today. It'll cost me nowt – in fact, I might even make a bob or two and it's a change for the lads. If we find Aaron's dog, that'll be a bonus for us all.'

'Do the lads down there know what's going on?'

'Aye, they do. I needed summat to stir 'em into working away from their usual spot. They won't tell awd Aaron though.'

My last visit that day was just before five o'clock, and the men were packing up. Aaron was talking to Jim Fairburn as I approached them.

'Any luck?' I asked Jim, a question that was open to more than one interpretation.

'Nowt,' he said, turning to Aaron. 'That dog o' yours must be well away under that limestone, Aaron. We've not seen it.'

'Are you working here tomorrow?' Aaron asked Jim.

'Aye, we've a lot more testing to do; I reckon this quarry's got a lot of good stuff left.'

'I allus said it had,' beamed Aaron. 'I said this quarry was one of t'best in this district, workable for years to come. Can I come tomorrow?'

'Sure, you'll be welcome.'

I took Aaron home and he was dejected.

'Them young fellers know nowt about quarrying,' he said speaking almost to himself. 'It's all blast and ignorance these days. No skill. I could show 'em a thing or two, but yon boss feller said I had to keep away. If you hadn't told 'em about Pip being in there, Mr Rhea, I reckon they'd have blown the whole bloody cliff-face down.'

'They've got to assess the depth of the usable stone,'

I tried to sound convincing, 'but they're being very careful about it, because of Pip.'

'Aye, they are. I appreciate that, Mr Rhea.'

'You'll be going back tomorrow?' I put to him.

'Aye, I will.'

I left him and promised to give him a lift in the morning, but he said he would walk. I decided to pop into the quarry anyway, and made several visits during the day. The work continued and, in my inexperienced eye, it was exactly like a normal day's quarrying. The layman would not have guessed they were seeking a little dog, and I wondered if the modern techniques were sufficiently changed to confuse the old man.

But at the end of the second day, Pip had not been found. I walked into the quarry at five o'clock and found Jim Fairburn closing the day's work. Aaron was deep in the workings, just standing and staring at the quarry face.

'I reckon that dog's dead,' Jim said. 'We've not heard anything, Mr Rhea. Jack Russells will bark, you know, if they hear anything. That dog's gone, I reckon. There's not been a whimper.'

'You'll not be coming back tomorrow?'

'Sorry. We've done all that we can – I've had the lads blast open all the routes we can find, and it's served my purpose. There is a bit of quarrying left here, but not a lot. Maybe a year's work for us, no more, but it would need equipment being here all the time. I've done what I wanted, Mr Rhea, but I haven't found old Aaron's dog. I'm sorry about that – we all are.'

'You couldn't have done any more.'

'You'll take him home?'

'Yes,' I promised.

I had my own car today because I was off duty, and gave Aaron a lift to his front door. He never spoke during that journey, and I knew he feared the worst.

'There's hope yet, Aaron,' I said as he left me.

'They've shifted more stuff in two days than we could in a week,' he sniffed, 'and still he's not come out. He is in there, Mr Rhea, I'm sure of it.'

'I'm sure you're right, Aaron, and if those men didn't find him dead, then there must be hope. He could live off things he finds – rabbits and so on.'

'Aye, but he would have barked, you know. He's bred to bark.'

'Maybe he was too far away for us to hear? You said those cracks went for miles underground.'

'They do, they do, Mr Rhea. Look, thanks for what you've done. Do you think I should write a letter to that Mr Fairburn, to thank him for looking?'

'I think he would like that, Aaron,' and he went indoors, closing the door behind himself. I felt sad; he had lost a friend, but dogs had survived longer than this underground. There was still hope.

Two days later, I saw him walking up to the quarry, his knapsack on his back, and a long stick in his hand. I stopped for a brief chat, and discovered he was going to shout into some of those cracks and fissures, just in case. He was going to spend the day there, he said. It was now half past eight and I was on my way to Malton for a meeting with the Superintendent; it was the quarterly meeting for rural beat constables and would take all day.

I returned past the quarry at about quarter to five, and decided, on impulse, to see if Aaron was still there. I guided the Francis Barnett down the rough road and leaned it against the office building. Aaron was positioned in the floor of the quarry, sitting on a large lump of rock, and he was eating a sandwich.

'Hello, Aaron,' I said. 'Any luck?'

His face told me the obvious answer. He shook his dusty old head and I said, 'Come along, I'll give you a pillion ride home.'

'No, Mr Rhea,' he said. 'I'll stay till dark.'

The tone of his voice indicated he had made up his mind, and I knew better than to suggest any alternative.

'I'll bring a flask for your supper then,' I laughed.

'He's still in there, Mr Rhea, you know. Alive. I can feel it.'

'I hope you're right, Aaron,' and I left him to his vigil.

As dusk was falling that night, I returned to the quarry with a flask of Mary's coffee and a round of ham sandwiches. I was in my own car this time, and drove it into the quarry floor. Even now, it was almost dark, and I could see the dim figure of Aaron Harland on the rock in the centre of the floor. I walked across with the food and drink, and his face revealed his gratitude.

'Anything?'

He shook his head.

'Here,' and I pushed the sandwich at him. He thanked me and ate it as I sat beside him, holding the flask.

'I'll drive you home, Aaron, you can't sit here all night.'

'If he is down one of those long cracks, Mr Rhea, he might hear us, but we might not hear him, on account of his good hearing, eh?'

'Yes, I'm sure you are right, Aaron. I'm not sure how sound travels along underground passages.'

'It echoes a bit – come, I'll show you before I go home.'

Leaving the flask on the rock, he took me to one of the large fissures and said, 'This is a new one, those fellers uncovered it with their blasting,' and he leaned into it, cupped his hands about his mouth and produced a piercing whistle.

There must have been a huge hollow chamber a long way inside, because his whistle echoed as he said it would. It was a faint, distant echo.

'If those chaps had blasted right back, we might have discovered a new cave system, Mr Rhea. There are caves hereabouts, you know.'

'Yes, I know. This place is riddled with tunnels and caves – I'd love to explore this area underground.'

We turned to walk away and in a moment of lovely silence, I heard the whimpering of a dog. It was faint, but it was there echoing down the passage. Aaron, with his ageing ears, had missed it.

'Aaron!' I halted him. 'Sssh …' and I held up my hand.

'What is it?'

'Listen!' I pointed to the gaping entrance of the fissure, but there was nothing. I waited with my heart pounding, and then I said, 'Whistle again, like you did.'

'It's the whistle I give when he's a long way off,' he told me.

'Fine, just do it!'

He produced the same piercing whistle and together we waited. And then, deep from the black recesses, we heard the unmistakable whimper of a dog.

'He's there, Mr Rhea, he's there …' and the old man jumped up and down and clung to me, with tears unashamedly tumbling down his cheeks.

'Keep whistling,' I pleaded. And he did.

The whimpering continued, but it grew louder. We waited a long time. The darkness was almost complete so I went to the car for a torch, and shone it deep into that ragged fissure. And there, hauling himself towards us, bruised, battered and dirty, was the unmistakable figure of Pip.

'There he is, Aaron,' I cried.

Aaron called him, and the gallant little dog literally dragged himself by his forelegs along the uneven, rocky floor of that crack. But he was alive …

Three days later, I called again. Pip was lying on the rug near the fireside, and he looked clean and well. His bright eyes surveyed me and his tail thumped the rug.

'The vet says he'd been in a fall of rock, Mr Rhea, and got badly bruised about his back end. He'd not eaten either. He's got a few cuts and bruises, but he'll mend. The vet reckoned another day down there would have fettled him.'

'I'm pleased you found him then.'

'Nay, them fellers who did the quarrying, they found him. That was a new crack he came along. I reckon if they hadn't opened it up, I'd have lost him.'

'It doesn't matter now, you've got him back.'

'Aye, I have, Mr Rhea. Isn't life grand?'

'It is,' I agreed, 'and you'll not be going back to Thackerston Quarry in a rush!'

'I am!' he said. 'I'm going up there tomorrow with my shovel and I'm going to block the entrances of all them cracks. I don't want any more dogs getting stuck in there.'

'It'll be just like going back to work, eh?'

'Aye,' he said, 'It will, but Pip's not coming this time! He can stay and guard the house instead. He can work at that for a change.'

I left him caressing the velvety black ears of his happy friend.

Chapter 5

'He is a portion of the loveliness which once he made
more lovely.'
PERCY BYSSHE SHELLEY (1792–1822)

IT WAS IN THE 1950s that litter gained publicity as a
problem in the countryside. This coincided with the
discovery of beauty spots by motorists and the post-war
fetish for putting things in near-indestructible plastic
wrappings and containers. When this kind of perpetual
rubbish is abandoned in picnic areas, woods, fields and
hedge-bottoms, it is destined to remain for eternity, if it
is not eaten by a cow.

If a cow attempts to eat a plastic bag, it will probably
block the cow's windpipe and kill it; if a hedgehog gets a
plastic carton stuck on its head, it cannot feed and will
die of starvation, and if an animal cuts its feet on a
broken glass bottle, it may survive for a while in acute
agony. Apart from many reasons of this kind, rubbish is
unsightly, messy and a confounded nuisance to country
people.

It cannot be disputed that some visitors to the North
Yorkshire moors and dales do cause litter problems;
some of their rubbish is little more than discarded orange
peel or cigarette packets, but others leave behind the
offal of their riotous weekends in caravan or tent, and
there are awful types who drive to the country for the

sole purpose of depositing unwanted domestic junk. Things like old refrigerators, mattresses and settees have been left in our woods and glades, and the snag is that these lovely areas belong to some unfortunate person who is left with the problem of removing the stuff.

It is akin to a countryman dumping his unwanted and rusting machinery in a suburban garden, or casting his waste animal matter into someone's semi-detached rockery. It is a sad reflection on life that even today, many townspeople do not know how to conduct themselves in a rural environment, and some regard a National Park as nothing more than a glorified car park. Indeed there are times when countryfolk feel they are being penalised for living and working in these picturesque areas, but in spite of such anti-social habits many opt to suffer these penalties rather than exist in a wilderness of concrete and bright lights.

Litter is a product of carelessness, rudeness and a lamentable lack of consideration, so in an attempt to counteract this unsocial trait, several organisations began to think in terms of a Best-Kept Village competition. The countryside needed some form of publicity if the flow of junk was to be halted, and this movement coincided with the passage of the Litter Act, 1958. This statute forbade the dropping of litter in the open air and reinforced its provisions with a staggering fine of £10.

As a village police constable, I was notified of the new Litter Act and was exhorted to reinforce it when people threw cigarette packets out of cars, cast chip papers into gardens or dropped beer bottles in the street. The snag was that the Act gave no power for the police to demand a suspect's name and address, nor did it give us a power to effect an arrest if such a person was non-co-operative. It was really a toothless tiger.

What the Act did achieve, however, was that it drew the attention of public-spirited people towards the litter problem. From this, a crop of Best-Kept Village competitions spread across the countryside and all kinds of official organisations and magazines like *The Dalesman* arranged their own contests. Our village was not going to be left out, and so it was decreed by the elders of Aidensfield that the village should compete in a local competition.

In keeping with the prestige of such events, a committee was formed whose duty was to encourage active participation by village people of all ages and groups, but especially organisations like the Women's Institute, Parish Council, British Legion, Boy Scouts and the Parochial Church Council. For that reason, a representative from all the parish organisations was co-opted on to the committee, and I found myself nominated because of my law-enforcement expertise. It was reckoned I would know a little about the Litter Act of 1958, and I would have the ability to crack the proverbial whip when slackness was observed.

The competition for villages in our district was organised by the Ryedale Village Communities Association which expressed a desire that all villages in the area should compete. The prize would be a colourful trophy made in metal and positioned on top of a tall oak post. That trophy, plus a plaque for display in the village hall, would be awarded to the Best-Kept Village in Ryedale. The trophy and the plaque would belong to the village for all time.

It was stressed that the competition was for the *best-kept* village and not the prettiest or the most beautiful, thus a very ugly place could win first prize if its residents kept it neat and tidy. The word was passed around the villages, nominations were sought, committees elected and a programme of judging established. We were told about it in February and discovered the judges would tour the competing communities in July and August. The winner would be announced during September, hopefully before the school holidays ended.

Our first meeting was in Aidensfield Village Hall on 10 February, which is Umbrella Day, a time for Englishmen to carry umbrellas in commemoration of the public's acceptance of this article. It was publicised by Jonas Hanway in the eighteenth century and he had the devil's own job to get the object taken seriously. I don't think the choice of this day was significant, but I never really knew.

The Chairman was Rudolph Burley because of his loud voice, and other members of the committee included the vicar, the Rev. Roger Clifton; the farmers' representative, George Boston; Joe Scully from the British Legion; Mrs Virginia Dulcimer of Maddleskirk representing local Women's Institutes; Joe Steel from the shop and me from the law, with one or two local folks to keep the villagers interested and involved.

Rudolph was a fine chairman, just as he was a good conductor of the String Orchestra, and after outlining the purpose of the meeting, he asked the committee to decide formally whether Aidensfield should enter the Best-Kept Village competition. Everyone agreed it was a good idea, and he suggested the vicar be appointed secretary to carry out our enrolment, and to fulfil future clerical duties. We all agreed.

'Right,' he said in resonant tones. 'I reckon we'll need one person to be responsible for each aspect of the contest. For example, the condition of the churchyard, and any burial grounds and chapel gardens is one of the judging points. I think the responsibility for that must rest with the vicar?'

He turned to peer at Roger Clifton who gave his consent.

Rudolph continued, 'Right, I'll list the points that will be examined, and if you wish to make yourself responsible for supervising one or more of these, please give your name. If I get no volunteers, I'll appoint someone.'

He paused to allow his words to take effect, then announced the first point.

'Absence of litter. Now,' he said, looking around the gathering, 'this is vital, of course. P.C. Rhea? It strikes me this could be your forte – you could always threaten miscreants with the Litter Act and the fierceness of our local magistrates!'

'I'll do it,' I volunteered and he wrote down my name. I found I was also expected to supervise the tidiness of the parish tip and other refuse dumps.

'Next,' he smiled, 'condition of the Village Green, Village Centre, and Main Street.'

Joe Steel from the shop felt this was within his province, especially as he walked the street daily to deliver his groceries and newspapers. He was also asked to supervise fences, walls and hedges, to ensure they were kept in good repair and in the case of the hedges, neatly trimmed. Joe was asked to make sure the residents kept their gardens tidy, painted their doors and windows, and removed junk from any shed windows which faced the street. Joe was also asked to be responsible for gardens and sheds which were within public view, although the judges would not enter private property. But whatever they could see would be considered part of the contest.

George Boston, being a farmer, was given the duty of chasing up the local farmers and their wives with a view to ensuring all farmyards were neat and tidy, with shovels, picks and all other implements carefully stored away or kept in graceful arrangements. Haystacks and rusty implements could be a problem, he was reminded.

Rivers, streams and footpaths on the outskirts were allocated to Joe Scully and he was asked to ensure that no beds were concealed under the bridge, and that old tyres, tins and rubbish were removed. The chairman did say he had noted a frying pan and three oil drums in Maddleskirk Beck and had noticed a nest of sticklebacks in a bean tin just below the stepping stones. The river must be as fresh as a mountain stream.

Mrs Dulcimer, who represented the Group W. I., said she and her members would see to the village hall and other public buildings, including the War Memorial, and they would also attend to the orderliness of advertisements upon local noticeboards. The Chairman pointed out that one notice in the anteroom of the village hall was still announcing the village's Coronation arrangements, and suggested it be stored in the County archives.

Every member of our committee was exhorted to co-opt the assistance of neighbours and friends and to use groups like the Boy Scouts and British Legion. We decided to adopt the slogan, 'Make Aidensfield Tidy', and make it the aim of everyone in the village.

There is no doubt that the enthusiasm of the Tidy Committee, as we became known, infected the villagers. In no time at all, the schoolchildren could be seen picking up rubbish on their way to and from the classroom, men in the pubs cleaned the streets as they walked home, farmers tucked in stray pieces of straw when they flapped upon their barns and old ladies talked old gentlemen into painting their doors, windows and fences.

Someone painstakingly picked the moss out of the lettering on the War Memorial and changed the poppy; the ivy around Ivy Cottage was trimmed, and Home Farm's milk-shed windows were cleared of their generations of spiders' webs and emptied of disused bottles of cattle medicine. The names of cottages were smartened up and their windows cleaned; door steps were given a coat of white when they abutted the street, and the shops arranged their notices in a tidy, artistic manner. One farmer even trimmed his horses' tails, and another painted a scrap plough because he couldn't be bothered to remove it. Milk churns were made to gleam and the parish seat was given a new set of wooden rails which were painted a pleasing green.

It is fair to say that the whole village worked very hard, more so because we learned that Maddleskirk, Elsinby, Ploatby, Briggsby and Crampton had all entered. We couldn't sully our reputation by letting any of them beat Aidensfield. But the work did produce its arguments, differences and examples of rural slyness.

In my role as the official Litter Eradicator, I made regular foot patrols about Aidensfield, trying to jolly the people along and constantly nagging at visitors and careless locals about the heavy fines for unlawfully dropping things in our tidy street and clean public places. It was during one of these foot patrols that I chanced to look into Ryedale Beck where it flows beneath Aidensfield Bridge.

To my horror, tucked neatly under our bridge, was the framework of a huge double-bed complete with rusty springs and an old mattress. It had been very carefully positioned because it was impossible to see it from the road, and it was by the merest chance I had noticed its reflection in the clear water.

I had to speak with Joe Scully, our man in charge of rubbish in streams.

'It wasn't there last week, Mr Rhea,' Joe assured me. 'I checked – I inspected every bridge in our parish. They was all clear, honest, so somebody's put it there! I'll bet it was the Elsinby lot!'

'Elsinby? That's a rotten trick!' I shouted.

'They're like that down there,' he said grimly. 'They'll resort to anything to get us to lose this contest. If the judges had spotted yon bedstead, we'd lose points, Mr Rhea. Points *and* the contest would go.'

'We'd better have it shifted then,' I said.

'Leave it to me!' he winked. 'I'll have it taken back to Elsinby at the dead of night. I'll cap 'em.'

'They'll know who's done it, won't they?' I reminded him. 'Then they'll only fetch it back when it's too late for us to move it.'

'Then leave it to me, Mr Rhea. I'm in charge of streams.'

I did. I saw him four or five days later and asked, 'Well, Joe, you managed to dispose of that old bedstead for us?'

'Aye,' he grinned. 'I took it down to Crampton and stuck it under one of their bridges.'

'I meant you to take it to the tip!' I laughed, 'not nobble the competition!'

But the deed was done, and I reported to the committee that saboteurs were abroad, so we must maintain constant vigilance. I did not tell the committee about the bedstead or its destination, but left a question mark in the air by saying I had received the tip-off about saboteurs from one of my reliable sources.

Our next piece of trouble came from Rufus, a golden Labrador dog with a lust for emptying dustbins. In the time I had been at Aidensfield, Rufus had been the catalyst of many fierce arguments because of his urge to push off the lids of dustbins large and small in order to scatter their contents over a wide area. Unfortunately, he continued this game during the run-up to the Best-Kept Village competition, and his owner had an awful time with him. Rufus got blamed for every piece of spare rubbish in the village.

The worst came one Wednesday morning. I received an irate telephone call from Mr J. C. Roberts, who occupied a bungalow almost opposite the house where Rufus lived.

I walked down the village to see the cause of Mr Roberts' complaint and when I arrived, I discovered a large sheet of newspaper stuck to his coalhouse door. The paper had clearly contained fish-and-chips at some stage of its history, and it was not a pleasant piece of rubbish. Also stuck to the same door was a margarine wrapper, a bread wrapper and a crumpled up piece of tissue paper containing some unmentionable goo. The finished result was a terrible example of modern art – 'Papers on a coalhouse door.'

'Look at that!' bellowed the irate Mr Roberts. 'It's that bloody dog again!'

'Rufus?' I asked innocently.

'Who else? He's upturned that dustbin at the house opposite, and last night's wind has blown those filthy papers on to my new paint. I'd just painted that door, Mr Rhea, ready for the judging and look at it now ...'

It meant another trip to see Rufus's master, who made his usual apologies, and I knew my efforts were wasted. I pleaded with him to keep the animal in close custody during the final days before judging. As it began next week, these final days were invaluable. Promises were made; Mr Roberts repainted his door and I hoped things would subside.

But they didn't. The next complaint I got was from a Mr M. C. Argument whose name was a perfect portrayal of his personality. He rang me at home one Sunday morning, and fortunately I was on duty. I called on him at ten o'clock that morning and he took me down his garden.

'Just you look at that, Mr Rhea!'

And there, in the centre of his lovely lawn was a huge pile of rubbish, clearly the contents of someone's dustbin. There were ashes, bottles, waste cartons, orange peel – in fact, a whole week's waste from a typical kitchen, all piled in the centre of his lawn.

'It's not yours, I assume?' I said inanely.

'It most certainly is not!' he affirmed with some feeling. 'It's that neighbour of mine. I've had nothing but trouble from him; he throws all sorts into my garden – weeds, junk ...'

'But never a full dustbin?' I asked.

'No, that's why I have called you in, Mr Rhea. This is the end. I've done my best for the Best-Kept Village competition, and this really is the limit. I have taken immense pains to get rid of my own rubbish and to keep my garden and house tidy – and then this!'

'I'll have a word with him,' I promised.

I walked around to the bungalow next door and knocked.

A pretty young woman with her hair all tousled and dressed in a housecoat opened the kitchen door and her pretty face crumpled into a puzzled frown when she saw me.

'Oh, I thought it was the papers,' she blushed.

'Mrs Fletcher?' I asked.

'Yes?'

'Is your husband in?'

'No, he's gone fishing,' she told me. 'Is something wrong?'

'Somebody has tipped a dustbin full of rubbish on to Mr Argument's lawn,' I said in what I hoped was not an accusatory manner.

She began to giggle and then clapped her hand over her mouth as she fought to control herself.

'Really?' she chuckled, showing good, firm teeth and a marvellous sense of humour. 'Who?'

'Your husband?' I ventured, smiling with her.

'Oh!' she came out of the house in her slippers and pottered around to a point beneath the kitchen window. 'It's gone!'

She pointed to a space on the concrete beneath the kitchen window and there was the circle of damp where the bin had recently stood. It had gone. I searched her small garden, and peered over the wall into the adjoining allotments, but there was no sign of the dustbin.

'Somebody's stolen our dustbin!' she began to giggle. 'Oh dear, whatever next. Why would anyone do that?'

'I'll bet it's one of the Elsinby lot!' I chuckled with her.

'They're desperate to win this Best-Kept Village trophy.'

'Do I have to report it officially?' she asked, clutching the coat about her slim body.

'Wait until your husband comes home,' I advised. 'He might know what's happened to it. He won't have taken it fishing, will he?'

She giggled again, prettily, and said, 'It was a brand

106

new bin too, Mr Rhea.'

'I don't think this is one of Rufus's pranks,' I said, wondering if she knew of the dog's delight, 'but I'll keep my eyes open.'

I left Mrs Fletcher and retraced my steps to Mr Argument where I acquainted him with the truth. When I explained that someone had apparently stolen the Fletchers' new bin and had dumped the contents on his lawn, he saw the funny side of it and laughed it off. I never did get a phone call from Mr Fletcher to make an official report of the theft, although I did keep my ears and eyes open for the phantom bin pilferer. He or she was never traced, and that mystery remains.

Another event during the run-up to the judging involved a weekend caravan family and a farmer called Derek Lightfoot. Derek farmed an expansive patch along the road between Aidensfield and Elsinby and at one point his land stretched well over a mile at both sides of the highway. He had several fields down there, one of which had a pleasing copse on top of a small mound, and this pretty area attracted passing campers and caravanners.

Derek had no objection to them camping there; often, it meant sales of eggs and milk, with a modest rental for the site. Some of his regulars came year after year, visiting the site over many weekends during the summer. But, in those final days as the Best-Kept Village contest produced its most hectic session of clearing the countryside, a man and his wife arrived in their caravan. They asked if they could park on this lovely little site for the weekend, Friday afternoon through to Sunday lunch-time. Derek agreed; he charged his few pounds in rent, sold them a dozen eggs and three pints of milk, and expressed a wish that they enjoy themselves. The man paid by cheque for everything, and thanked Derek profusely for his kindness.

During that weekend, Derek travelled past the site several times and saw the caravan parked half-way up his tree-covered mound. By tea-time on the Sunday it had gone. On that Sunday evening, Derek went for a walk with two of his dogs, and his route took him through the very same area. To his dismay, there was an enormous pile of household rubbish which had not been there on the Friday before the arrival of that family. It was more than a weekend's caravanning rubbish – it looked like a fortnight's kitchen waste.

It seemed they had loaded their surplus junk into a large plastic bag to bring here for disposal. There were empty soup and fruit tins, newspapers, a cracked bowl, a broken radio, several beer bottles, an old pair of trousers, two brassieres, fruit waste like apple cores and orange peel, paper, ashes and other household junk. It was a dustbin-sized heap and more, and it was attracting the undivided attention of the area's flies. Furthermore, tins with jagged lids and broken bottles were a hazard to both the wild and domestic life. Poor Derek stood there, with his anger rising. It was a terrible manner by which to repay a favour.

Even if the contest had not been running, this would have angered anyone, and Derek stormed home to ring me. Sympathetic though I was, I did not feel that the provisions of the Litter Act extended to private premises. It catered only for the dumping of rubbish in any place in the open air to which the public had access without payment. Derek's caravan site was not open to the general public, but only to a section of the public, and furthermore, he made a charge for its use. This meant I could not hope to bring a successful prosecution against the ghastly couple; in any case, it would not be easy to prove they had left it. Regretfully, I had to inform him that the rubbish was his problem.

'Aye, right ho,' he said. 'Ah'll deal with it.'

I saw him the following Friday as he trundled a tractor load of manure through the village. I stopped him to ask whether he'd sorted out his litter problem.

'Aye, Ah did, Mr Rhea. Ah capped that lot,' and he smiled knowingly.

'What did you do?'

'Well, they paid by cheque, Mr Rhea, and the bloke's name was on it. It was a funny name, with three initials. F. W. P. Oliphant, it was, and his bank was at Middlesbrough. Now there's not many blokes of that name, so Ah looked in t'telephone directory and found him. Ah rang him just to make sure it was t'same feller who'd camped on my land, and it was. Ah said he'd left summat behind, and seeing Ah was coming to Middlesbrough on Wednesday, Ah'd fetch it. So, you see, Ah went to Middlesbrough last Wednesday, Mr Rhea, and found his house.'

I began to guess what he'd done.

'Go on,' I grinned.

'Well, it was one of them neat little semi-bungalows, with a garden like a postage stamp. All neat and tidy, it was. Ah'd gitten all this stuff on my trailer and a good deal more besides, Ah might add, and Ah just tipped it all into his little garden. A whole trailer load, Mr Rhea. Mine, his and a fair bit from Aidensfield added in for good measure.'

'What did he say?'

'Nowt, Mr Rhea. He said absolutely nowt, and Ah just left. He can't take me to court under t'Litter Act, either, 'cos his is private land, like you said. Ah reckon more farmers and landowners should do this. Ah felt better after it, an' all.'

Unorthodox though it was, I had to admire Derek for his initiative and said I'd tell the story around the village, in the hope that others would take similar action against litter louts.

Then it was judging time. We knew the judges would arrive without warning and without identifying themselves, and so we worked hard to make our village spotless right through July and August. The schoolchildren helped by organising themselves into Keep Aidensfield Tidy groups during the holidays, and they set a wonderful example to their parents. It kept them occupied during the holidays too, and we maintained our tidy, litter-free condition well into September.

It was towards the end of September that Rudolph, in his capacity as chairman of our Best-Kept Village committee, received a letter from the organisers. It listed the points we had lost and gave the reasons, but then said we had won!

Aidensfield was declared the best-kept village in our area, and we were to be awarded the tall oak post with its lovely plaque on top. There was also to be a framed certificate to display in the village hall.

We had won by a narrow margin, beating Woodthorpe into second place. Woodthorpe was not on my beat, but it is a beautiful village on the east of Malton, on the way to Scarborough.

Needless to say we all celebrated, and then the big day arrived. The trophy was to be formally presented, and the committee decided it would be erected at the junction of the village street with the Ashfordly-Elsinby road. At that point, there is a small rising portion of land from which the sign would dominate the village and remind all-comers of our success. The Chairman of the Ryedale Village Communities Association intimated he would make the formal presentation on 8 October, a Saturday afternoon, and Rudolph was asked to make the necessary arrangements. All necessary publicity, and notification to the local Press, would be undertaken by the Association.

And so the great day dawned. Rudolph had organised a suitable hole for the pole and it was neatly squared with cement. Men from the village ceremoniously dropped the post into the hole and secured it, and then the speeches were made. There was a lot of cheering and pleasurable sounds from the assembled people, and I was pleased to see our triumph had attracted sightseers and villagers from far away.

By four o'clock, the ceremony was over, and everyone adjourned to the village hall for tea and cakes. I remained to guide a few visiting cars from the parking area, and as the last person left the scene, I noticed scores of ice-cream cartons, oceans of sweet papers, crumpled and discarded programmes and masses of empty cigarette packets which littered the area around our new trophy. There was rubbish everywhere!

Now that we were famous, visitors could come and drop their litter!

Unless it was the Elsinby lot dropping litter in pique...

So if you come to Aidensfield to see our trophy and admire our tidiness, please use the bin we've provided for your rubbish. It's the one marked 'Keep Aidensfield Tidy'.

One interesting outcome of the Tidy Village contest was the devoted attention paid to the churchyard. Before the contest, the churchyard had been neglected. There was no other word for it. The prolific grass between the graves was allowed to grow without hindrance, whilst many of the older graves had suffered total neglect. New graves did receive attention from relatives of the dearly departed, lots of them being attractively maintained and regularly replenished with fresh flowers. But as memories faded, so did the interest in these final resting places.

When a large area in a churchyard is neglected, the feeling is that the whole place needs attention, and for many years, this had been a problem for the Rev. Roger Clifton. He was too busy to spend his time wielding a scythe and his spasmodic band of volunteers cut the grass with enthusiasm for a week or two, and then became too busy themselves. The families of the recent and uncomplaining occupants of the graveyard tended their graves, and this resulted in a tiny, if changing, portion of the place being neat all the time, thus making the remainder look even worse.

It was the Best-Kept Village competition that changed the situation. In order to win, the churchyard must be groomed; the vicar did achieve great things on the run-up to judging because the grass was as smooth as a billiard table, and all the graves were neatly trimmed and supplied with fresh flowers. I do know that we received a very high mark for the quality of our churchyard.

The secret lay in ten sheep. They were black-faced moorland ewes owned by one of Roger Clifton's parishioners, Sam Skinner, and Sam had suggested there was nothing better than grazing sheep for keeping grass trimmed. He had volunteered their services free of charge, and had even offered to surround the churchyard's walls and hedges with wire netting to keep them in. During the first exploratory visits by the ewes, the fresh flowers were removed from new graves so that these highly efficient grass-cutters could get down to their real mission of shearing the thick grass.

There is no doubt they did an excellent job. Within a remarkably short time, the grass in Aidensfield Churchyard was shorn until it was velvety smooth, and even surplus weeds around the perimeter had been disposed of. Another of Roger Clifton's willing parishioners had built some wire netting cages, comprising sheep netting and wooden stakes, and these were placed over the new graves to safeguard the flowers and other graveside augmentations. These allowed the sheep to graze freely.

So successful were the sheep that it is fair to say they helped the village carry off the Best-Kept Village prize, although there had been some misgivings about the ethics of using sheep in such a hallowed place. The vicar rapidly side-stepped these misgivings by constantly alluding to shepherds and sheep in his sermons, saying these dumb animals were the Lord's favourite. The fact was the graveyard had never been so neat and tidy, and so it was decided that the sheep would remain at work after the contest.

And remain they did. Their presence kept the grass very neat, and the animals appeared to be content with their vital role in a human society. The local folks who had new graves to tend made good use of the portable, ewe-proof grave shields, and there were no further complaints.

Then at seven-thirty one Tuesday morning, my telephone rang. I was still in bed, having worked late the previous evening, and it was a struggle to stagger downstairs to take the call. But I made it, and in the meantime the whole family was aroused.

'P.C. Rhea,' I muttered into the mouthpiece.

'Roger Clifton at the Vicarage,' the voice said. 'Have I got you out of bed, Nicholas?'

'I was just getting up,' I lied easily. 'What's the problem?'

'My sheep. I mean the church sheep. Someone's stolen them,' he sounded very agitated.

'Stolen them?' I repeated his words in disbelief. 'Who'd steal ten sheep?'

'Lots of people get their sheep stolen,' the vicar remarked, and he was right. Sheep stealing was a profitable crime, especially on the moors where many animals were spirited away for handsome profits paid by unscrupulous butchers and hotels. Sometimes, a single animal was taken; sometimes dozens. I groaned at the news. A case of sheep rustling from the churchyard was the last thing I wanted.

'I'll be there in an hour,' I promised. There was little urgency with this. If the animals had been stolen, they'd be lumps of unidentifiable meat by now, and if they hadn't been stolen, they'd turn up somewhere else. I could afford to treat this alleged crime with a lack of desperate urgency.

I made myself a hearty breakfast before journeying down to the vicarage and I walked to give myself some exercise. I knocked on the vicarage door, and Roger Clifton answered. He was dressed in a casual sweater and light trousers, looking most unlike a man of the cloth.

'Come in, Nicholas,' he invited. 'Coffee?'

'No thanks, I've just finished my breakfast.'

We went into his cosy book-lined study and he seated me before his desk. I took out my notebook to record the details of this dastardly crime.

'Right,' I smiled. 'Tell me about the country's most recent case of sheep rustling.'

'You could be hanged for this, you know,' he said in all seriousness. 'Not many years ago, a man was hanged on the moors above this village, for stealing one lamb!'

'Nowadays, they take you to court, tell you to be a good man, and give you money from the poor box!' I agreed, 'so what's happened, Roger?'

'I checked my flock last night just before eleven,' he said. 'All ten were there. I counted them, as I always do.'

'To make you sleep better?' I said, but he failed to see the joke.

He continued as if I'd not spoken. 'And this morning, I went to unlock the church at quarter past seven, and they'd gone. I checked the whole place, in case they'd sheltered under one of the yews or even got into the boiler house, but there's not a sign of them.'

'Was the church gate open?' I asked.

'No,' he was adamant. 'No, it was closed.'

'There are no other means of exit from the churchyard?' I put to him.

'None,' he assured me.

'Did you hear vehicles in the night? Sounds of animals being moved?'

'Not a thing,' he said. 'There was nothing different this morning, except the animals had completely vanished.'

'"Go rather to the lost sheep of the house of Israel,"' I quoted from St. Matthew.

And Roger replied, smiling, '"I saw all Israel scattered upon the hills, as sheep that have not a shepherd."'

'Touché,' I said. 'So they've been stolen, you think?'

'What else can I think?'

'Let's take a close look at the fencing around the churchyard.' I had to say this. We police officers seldom take anything for granted, and I knew that a tiny gap in the wire was sufficient for these silly animals to stray through. And if one went, the rest would surely follow.

With Roger Clifton hard on my heels, I began my examination near the gate and turned right, thereafter following the line of the boundary around the large churchyard. Whoever had wired this before the judging of the Best-Kept Village contest had done a good job, for the wire was securely anchored to thwart adventurous ewes. As we carefully examined the western boundary, there was a tremendous bellow from the road behind us.

'Vicar?' came the shout. 'Are you there?'

That voice was unmistakable. It was Rudolph Burley, our loud auctioneer.

'Here, Rudolph, behind the second yew tree, with P.C. Rhea.'

We could hear the squeak of the gate as it opened and the crunch of heavy footsteps on the path. We waited until the bulky figure of Rudolph appeared.

'Ah, there you are! Are you looking for your bloody sheep, by any chance?'

'Yes,' smiled Roger Clifton. 'I think they've been stolen.'

'Stolen my Aunt Fanny! They're all in my garden, every one of those bloody silly animals, and they've eaten all my beans, my sprouts and most of my flowers!'

'Your garden? How ...?' spluttered Roger.

'I don't know how. I just know they're there, and I want them out mighty smartly.'

'Oh dear, I'll have to get Sam Skinner. They're his really, you know, just on loan to the church, and he'll drive them out. He has a good dog, you see …'

'There must be thick end of fifty quid's worth of damage to my garden, Vicar, and it's getting more expensive by the minute!' and he stormed away to protect his produce.

'You go and phone for Sam,' I advised Roger, 'and I'll check this fence right round. Somebody could have put them there for a laugh, you know.'

'Nobody would do a thing like that, would they?'

'Wouldn't they?' I smiled. 'Off you go.'

While he was telephoning Sam, I found the gap. There was a point where the wire had to negotiate some rocks and this created a fold in the wire; the fold produced a gap, which one of the sheep had located. It had widened the wire with its snout as it ferreted for fresh greenery, and very quickly had made a hole large enough to push through. The adventurous ewe had found herself at the other side of the hedge, the rest had followed, and all had made for some available and succulent greenstuff, which happened to be in Rudolph's extensive and beautiful garden. By first light, they had reduced part of his garden practically to the prime state of the churchyard, not a pleasant sight for a carefully cultivated corner.

'He's on his way.' Roger Clifton returned and we went around to Rudolph's to await Sam and his sheepdog.

Sam Skinner was a retired shepherd who kept a Border collie and several sheep as a form of active interest rather than for making money. He was an expert in all matters relating to sheep, and I watched as he entered Rudolph's garden, with his little dog at his heel and a long crook in his hand. As the dog saw the sheep, its ears pricked up and it looked at his master for guidance.

Sam gave a low whistle and the dog sat on its haunches, waiting for the next command.

'Where d'yer want 'em, Vicar?' called Sam.

'Back in the churchyard, Sam,' Roger Clifton said. 'With as little mess as you can make.'

'One of you ho'd this feller's gate oppen, and t'other ho'd t'choch gate wide,' he said. 'My dog'll do t'rest.'

As we went about our part of the operation, I heard Sam start to count the animals, and he used the old-fashioned North Riding dialect method of totalling them.

'Yan, tan, tethera, methera, pimp, sethera, lethera, hovera, dovera, dick.'

That was ten, and fascinating to hear. He waved the crook over their heads and whistled; the dog, with its head low, began to circle the assembled sheep and gradually rounded them up. Soon, they were a tidy group on the lawn of Rudolph's lovely garden, with the dog crouched flat beside them, waiting.

Sam checked that both gates were open, and with more whistles accompanied by the occasional gesture from his hand, he began to move the group, almost as one animal. They went towards Rudolph's gate as Roger waited, standing as still as a ramrod. The sheep hesitated before going through, but once one had made the break, the others would follow. Sam's dog encouraged the first to do this and seconds later, all were through and being guided along the lane towards the churchyard.

I held the church gate wide open and did my best not to alarm the oncoming flock. Man and dog, working beautifully together, guided the first through my gate, and in a matter of a few seconds, every sheep was back inside the churchyard. Very quickly, they lowered their heads and began to graze.

Roger came towards Sam and me as we waited at the gate.

'Thanks, Sam,' he smiled his gratitude. 'We couldn't have done without you.'

'Thoo'll nivver keep 'em all in there, Vicar, not now they've grazed all that grass off. There's nut enough for 'em all. You could do wi' only half that lot.'

'Is that so? Is that why they got out?'

'Could be,' Sam was non-committal. 'Maybe they were seeking summat fresh and juicy, like Rudolph's flowers.'

'Look, if you think five would be enough …'

'Ah do, and Ah'll tak five away right now,' and he whistled once more. The dog scuttled into the churchyard once again, and by using a complicated system of whistling, Sam ordered it to separate five sheep from the others, one at a time, and he gathered these in a corner.

'Ah'll away with them five,' he said. 'Mak sure that wire fence is sheep-tight, or they'll be out again. Who's going to pay Rudolph, then, Vicar? Me or you?'

'Oh, it will have to be the church,' agreed Roger Clifton, nodding his head quickly. 'Definitely the church.'

'Then you'll be holding a bring-and-buy sale for church funds, eh?' beamed Sam. 'Come, Rex.' At a further whistle, Rex brought five puzzled sheep out of the churchyard and Sam walked down the street, a happy man as the dog followed behind with yan, tan, tethera, methera and pimp.

It did occur to me that an outsider hearing him count the sheep might believe those curious words were the sheep's names. In fact, it is a very old system. The ancient Greeks counted in this way: 'Hen, duo, treis,

119

tessares, pente, hex, hepta, octo, ennea, dekem', while the Red Indians went, 'Eem, teen, tether, fether, fip, sather, lather, gether, dather, dix'.

As I pondered old Sam's skills, the Reverend Roger Clifton leaned over the gate and said, 'You know, Nicholas, it is a long time since we had a bring-and-buy sale for church funds.'

'Why not sell anything that's made from wool?' I suggested. 'Have a wool sale.'

'Nice idea; I might even get Rudolph to auction some of the garments!' he chuckled. 'He'd be very keen to raise as much as possible!'

'You could do worse.' I left him to his thoughts, and wondered how the shepherds of old counted up to fifty or a hundred. One day, I would ask Sam.

Chapter 6

'Blake is damned good to steal from!'
HENRY FUSELI (1741–1825)

IT WAS ONE OF those beautiful April mornings when no one in the world should have worries or cares. The sun was shining with more than a hint of the summer warmth to come, and the sky was a rich blue between the puffy white clouds which hurriedly crossed from one horizon to another. The countryside in Ryedale was a rich fresh green, with new foliage on the boughs and young buds desperately wanting to show off their blooms. There was a strong feeling of spring, both in my mind and in the song of the birds about me.

I was riding my Francis Barnett motorcycle across the hills into Ashfordly. I was not going upon any specific business, for it was one of those days when there was a lull in my daily routine. I had served all my summonses, seen all my farmers about their stock registers, checked all the firearms certificates that were due for renewal, and completed all my written work, including files on two traffic accidents and one case of housebreaking.

In my panniers, I had two reports which I was going to drop into Sergeant Bairstow's tray this morning, and then the rest of the day was mine. It was the perfect time to wander in bliss about the countryside. I would collect any incoming mail from Ashfordly Police Station – there might be some enquiries to make, or people to interview, but failing that I was free to tour the exquisite patch of England which formed my beat. I could explore new areas of my patch and meet new people, both vital to a village policeman. Local knowledge is so important, so this Thursday promised to be very enjoyable.

Ashfordly Police Station was deserted when I arrived. I let myself in with my official Yale key, put on the kettle for a cup of coffee, and set about removing my motorcycle suit. I would spend ten minutes here, sifting through official orders and instructions and checking the mass of crime circulars which came from neighbouring police forces. By the time I had removed my ungainly suit and dropped my correspondence into Sergeant Bairstow's tray, the kettle was boiling. I made a cup of typical awful police station coffee, flavoured by the powdered milk we used, and settled down at the counter with the file of recent legislation.

Then the telephone rang. Telephones always ring when one is at one's most leisurely, and I must admit I was tempted to ignore it. For one thing, Ashfordly wasn't on my tour of duty for today, so whatever the call was about, it was really the problem of the local duty officer.

But on the other hand, it could be Mary making efforts to contact me, or it could be somebody in need of urgent help ...

I put down my file, took a quick sip at the hot coffee and picked up the mouthpiece.

'Ashfordly Police,' I announced.

'Is that the police station?' demanded a loud voice. It was a woman and I got the impression she wasn't accustomed to using a telephone. By the sound of her voice, she didn't need one!

'Yes,' I said. 'Can I help?'

'My egg money's getting pinched,' she shouted.

'Egg money?' I groaned inwardly. Here was the report of a crime, so my planned carefree day had evaporated in a loud conversation.

'Aye,' came her stentorian reply. 'Egg money. Ah put it in my kitchen drawer and somebody's pinched it.'

'When?' I asked.

'Since yesterday afternoon.'

'And how much has gone?'

'Five pounds,' she shouted.

'And who is that?' I needed these facts for the initial record of this crime report.

'Blake,' she said. 'Mrs Blake, Laverock Farm, just out o' Gelderslack.'

'And your first name, Mrs Blake?'

'You want a lot o' personal stuff, Mr Policeman,' she bellowed, 'There's nut monny fooalks knows my name. I'm not one for gitting personal wi' fooalks.'

'I need it for my official report,' I shouted back. 'Then I'll come and see you.'

'There's no need to shout, Ah's nut deaf,' she said, following which there was a long pause before she added, 'Concordia.'

'Concordia,' I repeated, writing down the name.

'Aye, that's what Ah said.' She sounded embarrassed. 'But Ah'd rather be just Mrs Blake if you don't mind.'

'That'll do me. I'll come and see you about it. What time would be suitable?'

'Anytime will do me, Mr Policeman, Ah's allus about the place. If there's no reply from t'house, come and shout about the buildings. Will it be this morning?'

'Yes, within the hour,' I said.

'By gaw, that's quick,' and the phone went dead.

After completing my office work, my reading and my

coffee, I re-dressed in my motorcycle suit in case of April showers and locked the office. I didn't know Gelderslack too well, but enjoyed the journey because it took me from the floor of the dale high into the surrounding hills. Here, the countryside changed dramatically from the sylvan beauty of the valley to the rugged and rocky heights, replete with heather and bracken made happy by the song of the skylark. I had to stop at a cross roads to consult my Ordnance Survey map for the location of Laverock Farm, and found it along a lofty, rough moorland track.

The farm buildings nestled in a miniature valley of their own where the grass was green and the moor had not made any inroads. Mr Blake, and Laverock Farm's many occupants before him, had struggled over several hundred years to claim this piece of land from the moor, and it would be a never-ending battle to keep it green and free from bracken. If that farm was ever abandoned, the creeping bracken would envelop the cultivated patches and conceal them for ever. But now, it was a veritable oasis in this wild region, a memorial to the farmers whose work had produced it.

As I negotiated my motorcycle along the tricky route, I was not looking forward to this enquiry. It had all the hallmarks of what we call an 'inside job', more so when one took into consideration the isolated location of the farm. The theft of egg money was scarcely the work of an opportunist thief out here, and the disappearance of the cash must therefore throw suspicion on everyone who either worked there or lived there. Crimes like this always left a nasty feeling. The moment I began to ask questions, everyone would be under suspicion; they would suspect one another too, and I think it is fair to say that every police officer detests the thief who steals in this way. They are detestable because they steal, of course, but also because they cast doubts upon the honesty of everyone else in a small community or organisation.

I had to negotiate three gates before reaching the farmyard, not an easy task when struggling with a motorcycle on a track of this kind, but by eleven o'clock I was hoisting the machine on to its stand on a concrete area outside the Dutch barn. I removed my helmet and gloves, placed them on the pillion, then walked across to the house.

Although the whole complex was a little shabby and weather-beaten, I could see that it was clean and the fabric was sound; a coat of paint would have transformed the whole outfit, but its location in this tiny valley of the moors was delightful. As I walked towards the house, I could see the rim of the moors above me on all sides, while the sloping fields and bank sides beyond were rich with silver birch trees and conifers of various kinds. Somewhere out of sight, I could hear a stream rapidly flowing over jagged rocks, and a skylark sang in the sky above. Here was true tranquillity.

I knocked on the green door of the farmhouse and waited. There was no reply, so I opened it and shouted inside. Again, no reply. I remembered Mrs Blake's advice to shout in the buildings, and therefore began a tour of the farm, shouting her name.

She was in the missel, the local name for the cow-house, and responded by shouting, 'Aye, Ah'm coming.'

She met me in the doorway of the missel, a surprisingly small and compact lady with iron grey hair tightly curled about her head. She was barely five feet tall, with a fresh round face, and bright clear blue eyes. She was dressed in an old grey working jacket, known as a kytle in North Yorkshire, beneath which was a well used grey skirt and a colourful Fair Isle pullover. She appeared to be wearing lots of other skirts about her waist, but I think one garment was a hessian apron, known as a coarse apron, and another was her daily house skirt. I don't know why she chose to wear such a volume of skirts.

Thick brown stockings covered her legs, and on her feet she had ankle-length wellington boots and short, heavy socks.

I guessed she would be in her early forties, in spite of the grey hair, for she had a neat figure, from what I could see of it, and her eyes were youthful and very pretty. I tried to imagine her out of her rough, working clothes and guessed she would be very, very pretty, but I doubted if anyone would ever witness that event. I wondered if her husband had ever seen her in a pretty dress.

'I'm P.C. Rhea,' I announced myself. 'You rang me at Ashfordly.'

'Aye, that's me,' and she wiped her hands on a piece of rag before emerging into the daylight. 'Come in ti t'house.'

Off the telephone, her voice was surprisingly quiet, and she almost ran across the yard, with her little wellies twinkling at her rapid pace. She opened the door and went straight in, never halting to remove the dirty boots or any of her outer clothing.

'Sit down,' and she pointed to the plain scrubbed table.

I obeyed by pulling out a chair, and with no more ado, she set about making tea in a large brown pot which stood on the Aga in the corner of the kitchen. Then she produced a plate of scones and cakes. She placed all these before me, never asking whether I wanted anything to eat or drink, and I knew this was customary on the moorland farms. Any visitor, at any time of the day or night, was expected to partake of such hospitality.

Eventually, she sat in front of me, and smiled. It was a pretty smile, and beneath the rough exterior, there was a lovely woman. I wondered if she knew how pretty she could be?

'By, you got here quick!' she smiled. 'Ah'd hardlings got yon telephone put down when Ah heard that bike o' yourn.'

'Luckily I had no other commitments,' I said. 'Now, you are Mrs Blake?'

'Aye, that's me. And none o' that Concordia thing, think on!' she blushed just a little. 'If anybody calls me by my first name, it's Conny, nowt else. Just Conny.'

'I think Concordia's a nice, unusual name,' I commented.

'Well, you might, but Ah don't.' She picked up a scone and started to eat. 'Now, what do you want to know, Mr Policeman?'

'This egg money, where did it go from?'

'This drawer, right here,' and she pulled open one of the drawers in the table we were using. From my seated position at the other side, I could see it contained a good deal of cash, as well as bills, receipts and other bits of paper.

'You mentioned five pounds,' I reminded her.

'Aye, that's the one Ah'm sure about.'

'And when did it vanish?' I took out my notebook and began to tabulate the facts I needed.

'Sometime yesterday.'

'Morning or afternoon?' I tried to localise it a little more.

'After eight in t'morning and before tea-time – half-

127

past four.'

'You're sure?'

'Ah's positive!'

'And it was definitely five pounds? Was it five one pound notes, or a single five pound note?'

'Five separate pound notes, Mr Policeman. I know, because I put a pencil mark on their corners, all five of 'em.'

'Then some money's gone before?'

'Well, Ah wasn't exactly sure about that. Ah've been having a feeling for a week or two that my egg money's been going, and my husband said he wasn't helping himself, nor was that lass who works here.'

'Your husband? He's out today, is he?'

'Aye, he's gone across to Thirsk mart with some cattle. And this lass comes three days a week, Mondays, Wednesdays and Fridays, to do the house and a bit of work outside.'

'Who is she?'

'She's called Katy. Katy Craggs.'

'Is she a local girl?'

'From Whemmelby. Her husband has a small spread up there at Foss End, and she comes to work for me, to earn a bit. Two kids, she has, an' all.'

'How old is she?' I asked.

'Middle twenties, Ah'd say. Nice lass, a good worker.'

'Honest?' I had to ask.

'Oh, aye, dead honest. She's never done owt that would cause me to worry, Mr Policeman.'

'And your husband? Would he take any money for the mart, or his expenses?'

'Not without leaving a note in here, or telling me. Ah've asked him about this and he's not got it. If he had, he would tell me. He said Ah should call you fellers in.'

'Does anyone else work here?' I put to her, helping myself to another buttered scone.

'No, just us.'

'And regular callers? Do folks call here?'

'Not a lot. Hikers pass along that ridge near where you came down, and sometimes we get a salesman or two.'

'Neighbours then?'

'T'nearest must be half a mile away, and he allus comes on a tractor, so Ah'd know when he came.'

'Before I start making enquiries,' I adopted my official tone, 'I'll have to be certain, in my own mind, that the money is being stolen.'

'Ah wouldn't have troubled calling you if it wasn't,' she said solemnly. 'Ah wanted to be certain in my own mind first.'

'You've told your husband of your suspicions?' I asked.

'Oh aye, he said Ah should call in your chaps.'

'And the girl?'

'Katy? Nay, Ah've never voiced anything to her, not about getting t'police in.'

I paused, knowing that the girl would have to be interviewed, either to ascertain whether she was the thief, or whether she had seen strangers or indeed anyone else around the farm on Wednesday. The other alternative was to say nothing to the girl, and to set a trap.

My pause for thought caused Mrs Blake to look at me carefully, and then say, 'Now, Mr Policeman, don't say you suspect that lass!'

'I don't suspect anybody in particular,' I said, 'I was just wondering which was the best way to tackle this.'

'There must be somebody out there who creeps in when Katy's doing upstairs or cleaning the milk things,' was Mrs Blake's assessment.

'I think a trap is the answer,' I said after hearing this remark.

'What sort of a trap?' I could see the horror on her face and realised she'd be thinking in terms of rat-traps or rabbit snares, or even those huge, iron-jawed mantraps that were so popular in Victorian times.

'I don't mean anything that will hurt the thief!' I stressed. 'We can coat the money in the drawer with a powder that reacts to fluorescent light. If it is stolen, we can examine all the suspects and see if their hands have touched your money.'

'Oh, Ah see. Aye, well, Ah reckon that'll be all right. When would you want to start?'

'If the money's been going each Wednesday, we'll have to come next Tuesday and set it up.'

'Ah'll be in.'

'Don't tell a soul about this, except your husband,' I added as an afterthought. 'Once that money is marked and put in the drawer, neither you nor he will have to touch it.'

Conny Blake said she understood, and I promised to return to the farm the following Tuesday, with a detective to begin our operation.

We arrived about four thirty that afternoon, and enjoyed more scones, cakes and tea before planting twenty pounds in the drawer, in mixed notes, all of which were recorded in our notebooks by their serial numbers. Each one had been treated with magic powders provided by our Criminal Investigation Department. If anyone touched the money, the powder would transfer to their hands, and under the searching rays of an ultra-

130

violet light, the powder would show upon their hands, even after several days of washing. The suspect would never know the evidence was upon him. This simple but effective method is used to trace thieves who prey on their fellow workers or who rifle jackets or handbags in toilets and changing rooms. It is ideal for trapping petty thieves who operate from the inside.

We left Conny and her strong silent husband that Tuesday evening, with instructions not to tell a soul; they must not touch the money, and were told to ring me on Wednesday night if the notes had disappeared.

They didn't tell a soul, and the money did disappear. Another five pounds in £1 notes vanished sometime on Wednesday, so Conny rang me at home.

My first job must be to interview Katy Craggs. She must be seen, if only for elimination purposes. I did not tell Conny of my immediate plans but said I had a little initial enquiry to make and would visit them later in the evening.

It took me three-quarters of an hour to ride the Francis Barnett from Aidensfield to Foss End at Whemmelby, and as I parked my motorcycle against the drystone wall which bordered this smallholding, a young, dark-haired woman was hanging baby clothes on the line, to dry in the fresh mild breeze of these pure heights. She smiled as I approached, and waited happily in the garden as I opened the latch gate. I was not going to like this interview.

'Hello,' she smiled, as fresh as the April breeze which caressed my face, 'You're new, aren't you?'

'I'm from Aidensfield,' I told her, trying not to be over affable at this stage. 'I'm P.C. Rhea. Are you Katy Craggs?'

'Yes?' She was a lovely girl with jet black hair and eyebrows, and very dark brown eyes set in a pale, smooth face. She was well built if a little on the sturdy side, and had surprisingly large hands with rough fingers. I noticed these as she stood before me, clutching a bag of pegs and some tiny blouses.

'Look, this is not easy,' I began, standing at the gate. 'Is your husband in?'

'Terry? No, he's gone down to Brantsford to get some petrol. Did you want to see him?'

'No, it was you,' I began. 'You do work for Blakes at Laverock Farm?'

She nodded. 'I go there three days a week, yes. Scrubbing out, cleaning the bedrooms, looking after the dairy and working about the house.'

'You were there today?'

'Yes; is something wrong, Mr Rhea?'

'Yes, there is. Some money has been stolen.'

That awful look of discovery on her pretty face will haunt me for years. At first, her eyes and cheeks showed no sign of guilt, but within seconds her dark eyes had misted over and tears formed in the corners, to spill over and run down her cheeks. And her lovely, pale face coloured to a deep blushing pink. I knew she had taken the cash – now I had to prove it.

I continued, 'I must ask you if you have taken any money, without authority, from Mrs Blake's kitchen drawer?'

'You'd better come in,' and she wiped away a tear, using the child's blouse clutched in her right hand.

I ducked as I entered the low door of the cottage, and she led me into the kitchen. It was small and dark, for it was located at the back of the house in the shadow of the hill, but it was clean and tidy. She almost collapsed on to a kitchen chair, so I took the washing from her and placed it on the draining board.

I sat down beside her.

'Well?' I asked, not wishing to take advantage of the situation to make the girl feel any worse than she did.

She nodded.

'Look,' she said, 'I had to, for the children. I only get £2 a week from Terry ... two pounds to feed the bairns, clothe them, buy groceries ... I went to work to earn more, but he takes it off me for the car and his nights out...'

She broke down and told me everything. The children were in bed, and I think her husband must have remained in Brantsford to have a drink. I obtained a long, signed statement from Katy who admitted stealing £5 a week from Mrs Blake's egg money over some six weeks. I also included the reasons for her thefts and made sure the statement contained details of the money from which she had to feed and clothe her little brood. At that time, a reasonable week's wages was around the £15 to £18 region.

I took possession of today's five £1 notes, and gave her a receipt for them; there had been no need for the fluorescent light test, although I felt the sergeant might want to put these notes under the light to prove they had come from Laverock Farm, and that Katy had taken them, should she later retract her confession.

I cautioned Katy in official tones and told her she was not being arrested, because there was no need. I would proceed by summons instead; in due course, she would receive a summons to attend Eltering Magistrates' Court, when she would be charged with stealing £5 from Laverock Farm.

'What will happen to me?' she sobbed.

'It's hard to say, but I think you'll be put on probation,' I said. 'Now, I think you need assistance and advice. I will ring the local probation officer tomorrow, and get them to come and see you. Will you be in?'

'Yes, the children will be here …'

'I'll tell Mrs Blake next.'

'She'll sack me …'

'I'll tell her the reason. Look, this is not the end of the world, Katy, and there is a lot of professional help and advice available. Now, what about your husband?'

'He'll probably half kill me!'

'Shall I stay and tell him?'

'No, thanks all the same. I'd rather do it myself.'

She was gathering herself together, and I said, 'If you'd asked Mrs Blake, she'd have loaned you the money …'

'I don't borrow, it gets people into debt and needs repaying …'

'Are you going to be all right if I leave you?' I asked, knowing that some women would resort to tablets or other drastic solutions in a situation of this kind.

'I'll be all right,' she said, and because I believed her, I left the house.

Mrs Blake was horrified. The news hit her terribly hard, and she said if she'd thought it was Katy, she wouldn't have called the police. She'd have talked to the girl, to see if she needed help.

'Look, Mr Policeman, can this be stopped? Ah mean, does she have to go to court?'

'I'm afraid she does,' I said. 'Once a crime is officially reported to us, we must follow the procedure which is laid down. I am going to ring the probation service about Katy, because she does need help.'

'Ah've a few friends in high places too, Mr Policeman, and Ah'll get her sorted out. Ah'll go and see her tonight; her job's safe, by the way. She's a grand lass is that, and she shouldn't let that husband of hers ruin her like he has.'

'I agree entirely,' I said.

To complete the story, Katy appeared at Eltering Magistrates' Court, charged with larceny of £5 from Mrs Blake, and Mrs Blake came to speak in defence of the girl. The probation service was represented too, and told the story of her hardship; her husband bravely came to court in his best suit and said he had no idea housekeeping cost more than the money he'd been giving her. He now gave her £10 a week, and paid the electricity, the coal, the rates and the rent of his smallholding.

After hearing the case, the Magistrates wisely gave Katy a conditional discharge for the larceny, the conditions being, (a) that she repaid the £5 which was no trouble because the money was available after being shown in evidence, and (b) that she agreed to being placed on probation for a year. She agreed to both conditions.

I watched them leave court, Katy, her husband and her employer, all friends, and all wiser through Katy's offence. There is no doubt it was totally out of character, and that it was her cry for help. In her case, it succeeded.

I saw her several weeks later, shopping in Brantsford, and stopped her. She looked very sheepishly at me, but when she saw my mission was one of concern, she smiled.

'We're all fine, thank you, Mr Rhea. My husband is lovely to me now, he is, honest. He really cares, and Mrs Blake took me back.'

'You've a nice future to look forward to,' I said, not being able to think of anything else. As I strode back to my motorcycle I thought of the words of John Gay, who wrote, 'One wife is too much for one husband to hear.'

It had taken drastic measures to make Terry Craggs hear his wife's call, but when he had been compelled to listen, he had responded. He deserves credit for that.

It would be around the same time that another theft caused us a few headaches. I went into Ashfordly Police Station around half past nine one Sunday morning because I had been instructed to patrol this lovely market town for a couple of hours. Sergeant Blaketon was away on a week's holiday, and P.C. Alwyn Foxton had caught a dose of influenza. Because the town was therefore short-staffed, I was brought in for the morning, and Sergeant Bairstow said he would cover during the afternoon.

But when I arrived at Ashfordly Police Station, Sergeant Bairstow was already there, and he looked very worried.

'Nick,' he asked in a very confidential manner, 'when did you last see the county bike?'

I couldn't answer immediately because I had not used the huge black bicycle for months, and then only once to rush into town to catch the post.

'It must be seven or eight months ago, Sergeant.' I knew it was a vague answer, but it was the best I could muster.

'It hasn't gone for repair, has it?'

'If it had, it would go to Watson's in Church Lane. It's the only place that does cycle repairs.'

'When you are out this morning, pop in and ask if he's seen our bike, will you?'

He dropped the subject at that stage, and within the hour, I popped into Watson's. Even though it was a Sunday, the small garage was open and a mechanic was lying beneath a car, doing something to its

136

exhaust pipe.

'Morning.' I smiled at Mr Jack Watson, the boss of this busy but small business.

'Hello, Mr Rhea. Quiet, isn't it?'

'For a Sunday, yes,' I agreed, 'but the trippers will start soon. The market place'll be full of buses and cars by lunchtime.'

'So long as they call here for petrol, I don't mind. Well, what brings you here? Pleasure or business?'

'It's always a pleasure to pop in,' I smiled, 'but this time our sergeant has asked me to make a little enquiry from you.'

'Summat serious, is it?'

'Very,' I said sternly. 'Have you got our bike? The official one?'

'No,' he said immediately. 'Should I?'

'I don't think so. Sergeant Bairstow asked me to see if it was here for repair.'

'Nay, Mr Rhea, it's not been here for months. The last time we had it in was when t'back wheel needed straightening up, and that was nigh on a year ago.'

I returned to the police station at 11.30 to make a point there, in case anyone called from Divisional Headquarters, and Sergeant Bairstow was sitting with the cycle's record in his hand.

'Well?' he asked urgently as I entered.

'It was there about a year ago, Sergeant,' I told him. 'A job on the back wheel.'

'It's logged on the card,' he said, 'and the last time it was used, according to this, was eight months ago. It hasn't been returned to HQ for scrap, has it?'

'If it had, that card would have been marked accordingly,' I told him.

'I've talked to everybody else about it,' he sighed.

137

'Alwyn was the last to use it, and he put it back in the garage, beside the car, and it was in good condition then. And that was eight months ago.'

'That garage is often left open when we're out in the official car,' I said. 'Maybe someone's borrowed it?'

'Who?' he asked. 'There's one at Brantsford, one at Eltering and two at Malton. We got rid of one a year ago, because we're motorised and you lads have motorbikes. That bike was kept in cases of emergency, like a broken-down car.'

'Are you saying it's been stolen, Sergeant?' I put the question to him.

'Now, Nick, dare I suggest a thing? Who is going to make an official report to acknowledge we've been careless at Ashfordly by letting somebody steal our official bike? Just imagine what fun the Press would have – to say nothing of other police forces!'

'Maybe it's just been borrowed?' I tried to sound hopeful.

'Without permission? We can't go lending official bikes without permission. Besides, if it was someone local, we'd have seen it around the town, wouldn't we?'

'What are you going to do? Shouldn't it be reported?'

'I'm not reporting it, Nick. Not me! I'm too long in the tooth to go around raising hares like that. Just pass the word among the rest of the lads and I'll do the same. We might see it up a back alley, or hidden in a field or something. Then we can sneak it back without anyone knowing.'

'Will you tell Sergeant Blaketon?' I asked.

'Would you?' he put to me. 'If old OB gets to know, the balloon will well and truly go up. You know what he's like with his rules and regulations. Everybody will be under suspicion of pinching it, or selling it to make

138

money. He'll have the CID in to make a full-blooded investigation, and all our lives will be miserable. No, Nick, for God's sake don't tell him.'

'He's bound to find out,' I said.

'Then let him. Let him be the one to make the awful discovery, and let him have the problem of deciding what to do about it.'

And so the matter rested, at least for a few days. All of us who used Ashfordly Police Station as our Section office spent our spare time seeking the elusive black police cycle, with its distinctive colour and size. Large black bikes, with POLICE written in white on the crossbar, are not easily overlooked, but we failed to recover this one.

One thing I could not understand was how its loss had never attracted the attention of the ever-vigilant Sergeant Blaketon.

His eagle eyes and passion for checking every detail of his working environment must surely have revealed this loss. But he was away, and we could not, or would not, ask him.

On market day the following Friday, I was again in Ashfordly, doing yet another of my patrols due to the absence of other officers, when the station telephone rang. It was the police at Eltering, our Sub-Divisional Headquarters.

'Vesuvius here,' came the distinctive gruff tones of P.C. Ventress. 'How's life, Nick?'

'Fine,' I said. 'It's market day here, so there's a bit happening.'

'Well, I've some information for you. There's more about to happen. Is Sergeant Bairstow with you yet?'

'No, he's due any minute now.'

'Well, tell him to be sure to be at Ashfordly Police

139

Station at 12 noon, will you? The Inspector's coming over to check the station inventory and wants Charlie Bairstow there to sign it.'

'Right,' I said and after some domestic chatter, I replaced the telephone.

When Sergeant Bairstow arrived, he exuded cheerfulness and pleasure, but this rapidly turned to misery and anxiety when I told him the news. 'Never mind patrolling the town, Nick, find the list and help me check it. And what about that bike, eh? What's the Inspector going to say when he finds out it's missing?'

I was unable to reply. I just did not know the answer. With Sergeant Bairstow, I carefully checked everything else, from typewriter to official car, and all were present, or could be accounted for. Except the bike. And it was eleven-fifteen now. Forty-five minutes to zero hour.

'Nick,' Charlie Bairstow said to me confidentially, 'before half-past eleven, you must acquire a bike. I don't care where it comes from, or how long we can keep it, but just get one. Right?'

'But, Sergeant ...'

'Bike, Rhea,' he said in a very official voice.

'Yes, Sergeant,' and I walked out on my errand of mercy.

There wasn't a great deal of time left to find a suitable replica of the station bike, and as I walked into the town I didn't know where to start. Then I remembered Watson's Garage and its cycle-repair business.

Jack Watson greeted me with a wry smile. 'Now then, Mr Rhea, still looking for that bike o' yours, eh?'

'No,' I said. 'Another one, just like it.'

'Have we a thief with a liking for black bikes, then?'

'Who said anything about stolen bikes, Jack?' I laughed. 'Now, do you know anybody who's got a big

140

black bike like ours? I want to borrow it.'

'Oh, is that it? Well, I haven't any, but the Council chaps have.'

'Council chaps? Which council chaps?'

'Round at the Highways Depot. They bought one off me years ago, a big black Raleigh like yours. It was supposed to be used by the lengthmen as they inspected their bits o' road, but it didn't really get used. It'll need a lick o' paint, I should think, but it was t'marrow o' yours.'

'Jack, you're a life-saver!' and I hurried around to the Council Depot. In the office, I found a man who lived in Aidensfield; I knew him as John Miller, and he was a quiet, shy man who kept himself very much to himself. In fact, this was the first time I knew where he worked, although I'd often seen him around both Aidensfield and Ashfordly.

'Hello, Mr Miller.' He looked at me and his face bore that look of apprehension that greets most uniformed police officers. 'So this is where you work?'

'Oh, er, yes, Mr Rhea. Yes, this is where I work.'

'I'm here on a peculiar mission,' I said to put his mind at rest. 'Have you got a large black bike here?'

'Black bike? Er, yes. It's very old and it's not used a lot.'

'That doesn't matter. Can I borrow it for the morning please?'

'Well, it's got flat tyres, Mr Rhea, and is not in very good condition. Rusty, you know. Lack of use.'

'That's fine, so long as it's a big black bike.'

'A clean-up would do wonders, Mr Rhea, an oily rag or something.'

'Could we borrow it then?'

'Well, you'll have to ask the foreman; he's in the

141

yard, but I don't see why not.'

'We just want to show someone what a police bike looked like, and yours is like the ones we use. Ours are all at Divisional Headquarters now.'

'Oh, well, I'm sure it will be fine. Yes, I'm sure it will.'

I went into the yard, found the foreman, and presented him with my proposal.

'Aye,' he said readily. 'Take it. Keep it, Mr Rhea, if you want. Nobody bothers with it here, we never use it.'

'No, that would not be allowed. It's Council property,' and I went across to the lean-to which housed the cycle, along with other machines and implements. It was certainly in an awful state, and I half carried it out.

The foreman ambled across to me. 'Where's thoo taking it, Mr Rhea?'

'Round to the police station. We're just borrowing it for the morning.'

'Stick it in that dumper, I'll run it round. Hop on yourself.'

I looked at the cycle. Its tyres were flat, the chain was rusted and the spokes looked unsafe. I would feel a real idiot pushing this dusty, rusty monster through the streets on Market Day, and so I accepted his offer. We lifted the rattling cycle into the square, dish-like container of the dumper, and he started the engine. I climbed aboard the little yellow machine and we sailed out of the yard in fine style.

We chugged through the town at walking speed, the strong motor causing the dumper to throb and jerk as it progressed, and the ancient cycle rattled in the carrier. I stood beside the driver's seat, and we must have looked an odd outfit; within minutes, we pulled up at the police station and I lifted out the bike.

'Thanks!' I shouted above the noise.

'Think nowt on it; give us a buzz when you want us to fetch it back.'

'Thanks,' and he was gone.

I half-carried the cycle into the garage, and was placing it against the wall in the position normally occupied by the official bike, when Sergeant Bairstow came in.

'Was that you aboard that thing, Nick?'

'It was, Sergeant, and I have found us a bike.'

'Is that a bike?' he laughed as he pointed to the rusty thing.

'I'll clean it up, Sergeant.'

'I think you'd better. Is this the best you could do?'

'It's the twin sister of ours,' I informed him. 'It'll pass the inspector's casual gaze.'

'I hope it does,' and he left me to find a rag. I started to polish the framework, and after twenty frantic minutes, no one would have recognised this as the junk I'd brought from the Highways Department. The ironwork had been covered with a thick layer of greasy dust and this had protected the frame; the wheels were the same and were soon restored to a fine chrome which glistened in the morning light. I oiled the chain, and borrowed a pump from the man across the road. My hectic session with rag and polish had transformed it.

Ten minutes before the inspector was due, Sergeant Bairstow came to examine my handiwork, and was pleased. The inspector came, did his tour of the premises, accepted what he saw and signed the record of our inventory. Off he went to Brantsford to do the same, and we all breathed a sigh of relief.

That afternoon, I took the bike back to the foreman. Now I was not worried about my appearance when wheeling it through the town, and he was delighted.

'By gum, Mr Rhea, thoo's made yon bike shine for us. Thoo can borrow it anytime!'

'Thanks,' I said, not thinking I would ever have to accept his offer.

But less than a month later, I was once again in the office at Ashfordly, when Sergeant Blaketon loomed above the counter. He looked bronzed and fit after his holiday.

'Good morning, Sergeant,' I stood up to greet him. 'You look as though you enjoyed your holiday.'

'I did, Rhea. Yes indeed. It was excellent. We took one of those chalets, a self-catering place, on the Cornish coast. Very cheap and very nice.'

'I must do the same sometime.' It wouldn't be easy, taking all our youngsters to such a place.

'Do that, Rhea. I can recommend it. Now, down to business. When I left that holiday chalet, I had to check its inventory with the owner, item by item.'

'That's done in a lot of those places, isn't it?'

'It is, Rhea, but it reminded me that I have not checked the inventory of this station for some time. I thought I would remedy that defect today. Now, I have an appointment at the Council Offices in twenty minutes, and I expect to be there an hour.'

'Yes, Sergeant,' my heart was thumping. Of all the things to decide to do! And with our bike missing … he'd spot it. Even if we substituted the Council bike, old O. B. would notice. Nothing escaped his eagle eye.

'Right, then. Get things organised for when I return. Say eleven thirty.'

'Yes, Sergeant.'

I had hoped, as I'm sure we all did, that Oscar Blaketon would return from his holiday feeling in a benevolent mood, but it had only made him more chillingly efficient. I could imagine him sunning himself on the Cornish coast, and thinking of new schemes for Ashfordly Police Station and its members. But there was no time to lose. I needed that bike again.

I waited until he walked around to the Council Offices, which were fortunately several streets away from the Highways Depot, and then hurried around to my friendly foreman. Once more, I borrowed the bike, and once more he ferried the machine and me back to the police station.

It did not require a great deal of cleansing this time, but I gave it a cursory rub for luck, then positioned it where the official bike should be. Having done this, I went into the office, made sure all the objects and equipment were present, and waited.

Sergeant Blaketon came back from his meeting looking happy and efficient, and said, 'Right, Rhea. Inventory!'

I passed him the piece of paper which listed all our equipment. He set off at a fast gallop, touring the station and its curtilage and ticking off the articles as he found them in order.

Finally, it was the turn of the garage. My heart began to thump and I tried to anticipate his line of questioning when he found the replacement bike. He ticked off the car, the bucket for washing it, and the hose-pipe. He checked the tool kit, the spare wheel, the first-aid kit and fire extinguisher, and went carefully through his list, ticking off the items.

I felt sure he would hear my pounding heart, as I waited for our ruse to be discovered. I closed my eyes as he turned to examine the contents of the rear of the garage, but he saw the bike, looked for it on the list and said, 'Bike. Here.'

And he ticked it off the list.

As he turned back to me, I saw a strange expression on his face. It was practically indescribable; I could not decide whether it was a look of utter pleasure and relief, or whether it was one of surprise. Sergeant Blaketon was not noted for showing emotion, and later, as I thought about it, I think he was very, very relieved to see a bike there.

If one had not been there, there would have been all kinds of questions and accusations for him to answer as officer-in-charge of Ashfordly Section, and I think he guessed there was some sort of skulduggery because he did not closely inspect it. That was contrary to his usual practices; he did not, for example, check to see if POLICE was painted on the crossbar, nor did he inspect the serial number.

For once in his lifetime, I felt he'd taken the easy way out, although I could never be sure.

But on the way from the garage, he said, 'You know, Rhea, I think you ought to be put in charge of the station bike. Then, when we have an inventory check either by me or by the inspector, you could make sure the bike is clean and well-maintained. Do you think that is a good idea?'

'Yes, Sergeant.' I couldn't say anything else.

Afterwards, it did occur to me to ask the Council foreman if we could keep the cycle at the police station, for safe custody of course, and then he could ask for it if his bosses ever wanted to carry out an inspection.

Chapter 7

'At once on all her stately gates
Arose the answering fires.'
THOMAS MACAULAY (1800–59)

POLICE OFFICERS SPEND A proportion of their time near fires, either watching the fire brigade extinguish them, or warming their cold posteriors in moments which are stolen from the critical gaze of the general public. By this means, they discover the truth of the old saying that 'If you wish to enjoy the fire, you must put up with the smoke'.

From their back-side warming moments, many officers steadfastly confirm the old legend about Noah sitting on a leak in his ark. If you don't know this story, it attempts to explain why men enjoy standing with their rumps on offer to a blazing fire. The story is that Noah's Ark sprung a leak, and one of the two dogs on board attempted to stop the leak by sticking its nose into the hole. That brave act has since been commemorated by all dogs, because they all have cold noses. However, the leak became so large that the puny nose of the dog was too small, and so Noah offered to sit on the hole. And so he did; his stern endeavour kept the water out and since that time it has been the misfortune of male members of the human race to suffer from cold bottoms. For this reason, men love to stand with their backs to a fire.

Some fires, however, are too large for this to be done in comfort.

Of the unexpected fires attended by police officers, some are the result of arson, some the outcome of carelessness, some arise from accidents and many occur through sheer stupidity. The sources of some blazes remain unknown, or they arise through natural causes, but it is a fair comment to say that the discovery of an unwanted fire prompts urgent action by those who find it.

Here in rural North Yorkshire however, the definition of 'urgent action' is relative. What is urgent to a city man is not necessarily urgent to a countryman, and I had a wonderful example of this at Eltering Police Station one sunny afternoon.

I had attended court during the morning to give evidence in a case of careless driving. The sitting, with its list of miscellaneous offences, had stretched until lunchtime without hearing my case, so I enjoyed a quick sandwich and my flask of coffee in Eltering Police Office, as I waited my turn in the afternoon.

The office is neat and modern. It is part of a new complex of official buildings comprising the Fire Station, Ambulance Station, Court House and Police Station. All are housed within this pleasantly built and conveniently situated block of buildings with its tree-lined forecourts and tubs of geraniums.

It follows that there is a good deal of coming and going by members of the public. One pleasing fact is that visitors regularly pop into the police station for nothing more than a chat or to pass the time of day. It is a friendly place. The officer on the counter is content to while away his hours in the same way, there being little else to worry him. Such is the pace of life at Eltering.

That lunchtime, therefore, I was seated at a small desk at the rear of the enquiry office, and Vesuvius, the gentle giant of Eltering Police Station, manned the counter. As I munched my lettuce sandwich, he was gazing out of the window, contemplating life.

'Hello,' I heard him say to himself, 'There's awd Reuben Tempest on his tractor.'

I paid slight attention to his remark, for I did not know Reuben Tempest, nor did I know why his presence on a tractor was worthy of comment. Soon, the air was filled with the throbbing notes of his tractor as it pulled up directly in front of the police station where Reuben switched off the engine. A few moments later, the office door opened, ringing the bell to announce the arrival of a customer, and a ruddy-faced farmer presented himself at the counter.

'Now then, Reuben,' greeted Vesuvius, rising from his chair. I didn't know which of them was the untidiest, for Vesuvius' uniform was crumpled and his shoulders were covered in dandruff; this new arrival was clad in an old yellow sweater with mud and dirt all over it, and his long, straggly fair hair was protruding at all angles from beneath his grimy flat cap.

'Now then, Alf.' The farmer addressed Vesuvius by his Christian name; his real name was P.C. Alfred Ventress.

'Grand morning,' returned Vesuvius. 'Aye, not bad for t'time of year,' said the farmer, looking at the day through the office windows. 'This year's passing along nicely.'

'You'll be farmed up, then?' asked Vesuvius.

'Coming along. Aye, Ah's coming along. Ah've gitten that 100 acre cut and dried and my turnips howed ovver. Mind you, Alf, there's a lot to do. There's allus a lot to do on a farm.'

'Nay, you fellers mak it all up. You're nivver busy, allus just pretending. You spend all your time at marts or sales, and get other folks to do t'graft.'

Reuben grinned. 'It's neea good keeping a dog and barking yourself, is it?'

'Nay, I'll agree to that. Anyway, what's up? It must be serious if you've rushed here on that tractor.'

'Well, Ah don't know whether it's summat I should rightly trouble you with, Alf,' the farmer pursed his lips and rubbed his chubby cheek. 'But my missus is out at Scarborough, and Ah didn't know who to ask for advice, so because Ah needed a drop o' diesel for that awd tractor, Ah thought Ah might as well pop into Eltering, and see you chaps at t'same time.'

'Summat serious, is it?' asked the policeman.

'Aye, we've a fire at our farm.'

At the words 'fire' my ears pricked up; this was serious. But for these characters, it wasn't serious enough to panic them or to rush into frantic action.

'What sort of a fire?' asked Vesuvius.

'It's a grass fire,' the farmer told him.

'A big 'un, is it?'

'Oh aye, there'll be a few acres burning.'

'Do you want it putting out or summat?'

'Aye, well Ah think it might be best. Ah've been to have a look and it's on t'railway side, along yon cutting at t'bottom of my land. There's a wood doon yonder that might be at risk, and some buildings of Harry Tordoff's – he's away on holiday – and then there's them corn fields o' mine. Now, if yon blaze got among my corn, it would mak a mess of my harvesting.'

'You've got your hay in though?' asked Vesuvius.

'Oh, aye, in and stacked.'

150

'It would make a mess o' them stacks then, if it got close enough?'

'It would that!'

'How long's it been blazing then?' asked Vesuvius.

'Nay, now Ah've no idea. Ah spotted it when Ah was having my dinner, so Ah went and had a look, and saw it was pretty bad, so Ah came here.'

'All of a rush on your tractor?'

'Aye.'

They paused in the middle of this remarkable conversation, and then Vesuvius asked, 'Did you ring t'Fire Brigade, Reuben?'

'Nay, Ah didn't. That's why Ah'm here. Ah thought Ah'd cum and ask if you thought Ah should.'

'It's nut a bad idea when there's a fire, Reuben. Those fellers are pretty good at putting 'em out if they're told about 'em.'

'Well, Alf, thoo sees, Ah've heard they've got to cum all t'way from Northallerton or somewhere. Noo that's all of forty-five miles and it's a long way …'

'Nay, lad!' soothed Vesuvius. 'Just because we ring 'em at Northallerton, doesn't mean they cum from there. When we ring 'em at Northallerton, they ring bells and things at Eltering, then our local lads turn out. Their spot is right next door, here, just along t'path.'

'Oh, that's how it works, eh? So if Ah'd telephoned from my spot, it wad have gone through to Northallerton, and they'd have rung t'lads here, and these lads would come and fettle my fire?'

'Aye,' nodded Vesuvius.

'Right, well Ah'll get away home and give 'em a ring. Ah'll etti be sharp because it's gittin a strang hold, is yon fire. It's moving pretty fast.'

'Noo, there's no need to panic, Reuben.' Vesuvius

was already lifting the receiver. 'Ah'll ring Northallerton now.'

Reuben stood by and watched with something bordering on amazement as Vesuvius used our private line to dial direct into the Fire Station; as Eltering Fire Station is manned by part-timers, his call went automatically to Fire Brigade Headquarters at Northallerton.

'By that was quick!' admired Reuben, as Vesuvius spoke.

'Hello, yes, Eltering Police here. I've a Mr Reuben Tempest with me. He's from Low Marsh Farm, Eltering,' he paused as the operator made a note of the name and address, then continued, 'There's a fire on his farm. A grass fire, and it's moving fast, and is threatening his crops.'

And Vesuvius replaced the telephone.

'Now, Reuben,' he said, 'Get yourself round to next door and wait for t'lads to come. They'll be there in a jiffy; tell 'em exactly where yon fire is, and then follow on.'

'Have Ah time to get my diesel, then?' asked the farmer.

'Nay, thoo has not!' Vesuvius said firmly. 'By t'time thoo gets around next door, them fire brigade lads will be there, anxious to be off. So get thyself there sharp.'

As he turned to leave the police station, the siren sounded above the town, and Reuben's ears pricked up. 'Is that it?'

'That's it, Reuben. That's Northallerton calling 'em to your fire, but they need an engine first, full o' watter.'

'And that's in t'garage next door to you, eh?'

'It is.'

'By gum, Alf, things is getting very official,' and he left.

I saw him pottering along the footway towards the doors of the Fire Station, and even as he left us the first fireman hurtled past on his bicycle. Within seconds, others arrived by taxi, car and motorcycle, all half-dressed in their uniforms, and all desperately anxious to beat their previous best time for getting mobile.

Within two minutes of the siren's awful notes fading into the summer air, the gleaming red fire appliance, with its bell ringing, tore out of town on its way to Reuben's grass fire.

I saw him climb on to his tractor, then turn in the opposite direction.

'He'll be going for his diesel,' said Vesuvius, returning to his books.

I learned that the fire was safely extinguished before it damaged any of Reuben's crops or buildings, although it left its mark on the grass embankment of the railway line. For Reuben, it was a moment of drama in his day, and I doubted very much whether he'd tell his wife about it when she came home. He'd probably tell her he'd had a few problems getting his diesel oil.

It is worthy of comment that in those days, every part-time fireman had a bell in his house. The bells rang to call them to the station, and these were supplemented by the noisy siren in town. When those noises occurred, the local people knew it was vital to keep clear the route from each fireman's home or place of work, for they knew that half-dressed men would soon hurtle through the streets aboard any kind of transportation they could find. To stand in the way of those dashing men was both dangerous and frustrating, and so the call of the siren meant the town's people froze until the fire engine was safely at its destination.

But modern technology has caused some problems.

Now, each fireman has a bleeper, and this makes a personal noise to inform him that his presence is urgently required at the fire station. The snag with this system is that no one else knows. The siren doesn't sound any more, and so the people are unaware of this impending stampede.

The result is, quite without warning, towns like Eltering are full of half-dressed men in cars and on bicycles hurtling through the streets on missions that appear bewildering.

One outcome of this new procedure is an increase in the number of traffic accidents in towns like Eltering, as people and firemen collide. As a form of communication, the old-fashioned siren had a lot to commend it – it ensured that everyone knew what was happening. And in a small community, that is important. But I often wonder what Reuben thinks of the new system – he probably thinks modern firemen arrive by telepathic means.

In that same summer, two old men of Aidensfield caused something of a panic when a henhouse caught fire.

The henhouse was totally destroyed, but because the blaze occurred during the daytime, all the hens were outside, pecking to their hearts' content in the small enclosure provided for them. The hens, and their ruined home, belonged to Arthur Poskitt who was one of the old men in question. The other was his life-long friend, Sam Crowther.

Friends though they were, the two old men, both well into their seventies, used to argue and fight over trivialities. This long-standing battle continued in their homes, in their neighbouring gardens and in the pub during an evening when they went for their pints of refreshing medicine.

The destructive henhouse fire was the outcome of such an argument. Long before I was posted to Aidensfield, Arthur Poskitt had owned a henhouse on the same site. It had been a smart construction of timber, well saturated with creosote for the purposes of preservation and for water-proofing, and it had a sound roof of equally waterproof material. Inside, there had been double perches, and nest boxes so that six hens could lay at the same time. In this comfortable abode, therefore, Arthur had kept a dozen Rhode Island Reds.

Then one fateful day, during a summer of long ago, Arthur's henhouse had ignited. The hens had been saved because they were outside at the time, and those who'd been inside were wise enough to flee the place as the flames licked their feathers. Most of the village thought this old fire had been forgotten – but it hadn't.

It was a heated argument over that first fire which caused the second. The second one occurred during my period of duty at Aidensfield, and the story happened something like this.

It was a long, hot summer day in July, when the whole of Europe, including Aidensfield, was basking in a heatwave of remarkable intensity. All over the place, girls in scanty costumes pleased the men by displays of beauty seldom seen in rural areas, and the men sat around hoping that the heat of the sun would not burn the hairs off their chests. It was one of those summers when it paid to remain in England, for the suntans here were better than those obtained at great expense in France or Spain.

Around twelve noon on the fateful day, the two old men were sitting in deckchairs just beyond Arthur's henhouse, with handkerchiefs draped over their heads, and braces supporting ancient corduroys which were rolled up to the knees. They were not asleep, although a passer-by would have had to be very alert to discern any sign of wakefulness.

The two old characters had been sitting in this semi-comatose position for several hours, when Sam spoke.

'This is like that day when your henhouse caught fire,' he said.

'It wasn't as hot as this,' came the reply.

'It was hotter,' Sam affirmed. 'Much hotter!'

'It wasn't as hot as this when my henhouse caught fire,' retorted Arthur. 'Nowt like.'

'I remember it well,' returned his friend. 'It was a damned sight hotter than this, because you needed two handkerchiefs over your head and you had sunglasses on.'

'That wasn't because it was hotter. It was because my eyes were tender, and my head was sore.'

'You never told me your eyes got tender, or your head got sore?'

'Why should I tell you? If my head gets sore, it's nowt to do with you.'

There followed a lengthy pause, after which Sam renewed the attack.

'You remember that day, then?'

'What day?' answered Arthur.

'That day your henhouse caught fire.'

'Remember it? Aye, of course I remember it. It cost me enough to build this new 'un.'

'It was your own fault.' Sam now scored a triumphant hit.

'My fault?' Arthur sat bolt upright in his chair, his old eyes blinking against the sun. 'Who said it was my fault?'

'They all did.'

'Who's 'all'?'

'Folks in Aidensfield. They all said it was your fault. You put your pipe in that long grass, on a day like this, and it caught fire.'

'It was kids what did it!' snapped Arthur, reclining once again.

'What kids? We were here, both of us. You and me. The kids were at school. It was before t'summer holidays. There was no kids, just us two, sitting here, and all that dry grass.'

'Well, it wasn't me. My pipe would never have done a thing like that. You don't set grass on fire with pipes!'

'You can! All you want is a pipe full of hot ash, and a bit o' wind, and dry grass'll catch fire like nowt.'

'Well, it didn't set my grass on fire, nor my henhouse.'

'There was nowt else!' Sam continued his attack. 'Summat must have set it alight. Henhouses don't catch fire themselves.'

Arthur sat upright in his chair once again and glared across at his reclining friend.

'Are you trying to tell me that my pipe will set fire to grass?'

Sam didn't move as he said, 'Aye. Remember – it was long, dry grass, nearly like hay, and there was just a touch o' breeze. You put that pipe o' yours down when you went in for a glass o' watter, and when you came out, yon grass was well away. Ah knew that and t'whole of Aidensfield knew.'

'Then you must have told 'em. There was only you and me here.'

'Then you admit it? You admit it was your pipe?'

'I admit nowt! All I'm saying is that a pipe full o' hot

157

baccy isn't strang enough to set fire to growing grass, no matter how dry it is.'

'Cigarette ends have set fire to forests before today,' Sam said with a nod of his head. 'And they've set fire to settees and houses, an' all. If a cigarette end can do that, then a full pipe can set fire to growing grass – and henhouses.'

There was another long pause before Arthur struggled to climb out of his deckchair.

'I'll prove it!' he said. 'I'll prove that a pipe full o' hot baccy can't set fire to growing grass. There's growing grass there,' and he pointed to a length of dry grass which grew beneath the hedge. 'I'll fetch my pipe and show you!'

'You do that!' and Sam waved a finger at his pal.

Arthur went indoors to find the pipe he hadn't smoked for years, and emerged with it, plus a box of matches and some ready-rubbed tobacco. He sat on the edge of his deckchair and studiously filled the pipe, pushing the dried tobacco deep into the bowl in readiness for its test. Then he lit a match, applied it to the pipe, and inhaled as only a smoker can. Even though he'd rested from his pipe for some time, he soon had the bowl glowing like a furnace, and clouds of sweet smoke circled above his head.

'That's a good pipe!' smiled Sam.

'Not one of my best,' Arthur told him, 'but good enough for this.'

'Good enough to set fire to a henhouse, eh?'

'Good enough for a test like this!' snapped Arthur, removing the pipe from his mouth and peering into its bowl. 'It's ready.'

'It'll be only right if you do today what you did last time you set your henhouse on fire.' Sam could not resist the gibe.

'This is to show my pipe couldn't have done it; now that time, I set it down and went in for a glass o' watter...'

'Then we'll do t'same this time, and I'll come with you, just to make sure you do everything ...'

Arthur's pipe was glowing nicely and he carefully set it down in the long grass, just as he had all those years before; it sat steadily between the dry stalks, a tiny glow of dangerous red among the tan colours of the weathered growth.

'Just like that, Sam,' beamed Arthur, pleased that his faithful pipe had not fallen over. 'Now, then, a glass o' watter ...'

Together, the pair of them marched in step towards Arthur's kitchen where Arthur, re-living as best he could the events of long ago, reached into the cabinet, found a glass and filled it with water from the tap.

'I think my missus asked me summat, but I can't remember what it was,' he said, sipping heavily. 'Then I went outside ...'

And he stalked back through the kitchen, round the corner of the brick cottage, and there, blazing furiously, was his patch of dry grass.

'It's afire!' he shouted. 'Sam, the bloody grass is blazing again! Git some watter!'

But old men are not as agile as they believe, and in the confusion and delay of those precious seconds, the searing flames were fanned by a fresh breeze which blew between the cottages. In a matter of seconds, the entire area of dry grass, which grew long and thick beneath the hedge, was ablaze and roaring towards the henhouse.

'Watter, watter!' shouted Arthur. 'Sam, ring for t'brigade ...'

'You ain't a phone!'

'Try t'Post Office!'

And so the pair of them tried to bring about an air of calmness and efficiency as they worried what to do next. As Arthur tried to find a bucket, and as Sam rushed off to telephone the fire brigade, I noticed the pall of smoke rising from behind the village street.

At first, it meant nothing special. The folk here lit many fires in their gardens to burn their rubbish, and this fire had all the indications of such a blaze. There was the thick grey smoke coupled with the scent of burning vegetation, and even from my vantage point in the street, I could see that the seat of the fire was well away from the houses.

It was only when Sam came rushing out of the gate, shouting, 'Fire,' that I knew something was wrong.

'What's up, Sam?' I asked.

'Fire, Mr Rhea, in Arthur's garden. Send for t'Brigade, sharp.'

'What's on fire?' I asked.

'Grass,' he said, 'but it's blowing towards his henhouse!'

I was torn between two immediate courses of action. At that moment, I knew nothing of the history of this event, nor did I know the geography of Arthur's garden, but I recognised the alarm on Sam's face.

'Right, Sam, I'll fetch a fire engine. You go back and try to put it out.'

The nearest fire brigade was a private one at Maddleskirk Abbey. It was run by the monks for the protection of their own premises and it comprised one Green Goddess and lots of pipes, all staffed by an enthusiastic band of monks who donned firemen's uniforms for the occasion. They liked nothing better than a local opportunity to practise their fire fighting craft. Besides, they'd be there a good half-hour before the part-time Ashfordly Brigade, and those minutes could be vital if Arthur's henhouse was at risk.

I rang the Maddleskirk Abbey Chief Fire Officer, otherwise known as Brother Laurence, and gave him brief details.

'Lovely, Mr Rhea, we'll be there in a jiffy.'

I marvelled that Brother Laurence had been selected as Chief Fire Officer, when his namesake, St Laurence of Rome, was invoked by religious folk everywhere to protect them against fire. St Laurence was roasted alive on a gridiron to suffer a martyr's death, and I hoped Brother Laurence would not come to a similar fate in Arthur's henhouse.

I hurried back to the scene and entered Arthur's garden through his small gate.

The two old men were using everything possible to extinguish the running fire which threatened the henhouse. The hens, in the meantime, had been cast out of their run, and the gate had been opened to permit entry by the fire brigade. I ran to them, grabbed a spade and started to beat the glowing grass, hoping to kill the flames. It was like fighting a forest fire – the tall grass was riddled with new seats of flame, and as fast as we put out one tongue, another erupted elsewhere. The three of us were kept busy, but it was no good. The running fire, fanned from behind by the strong warm breeze, had crept along the back of the part we were tackling. Those flames were concealed by smoke and vegetation, and were already licking the creosoted walls at the rear of the henhouse. None of us noticed them until it was too late.

Suddenly, the henhouse was roaring as the flames ate into the wood which was so richly fuelled for them; the dry timber, with its creosote coating, was a gift from the gods, and the blaze roared across that rear panel in a split second.

'Arthur!' I shouted, but it was too late. The ferocity of the blaze was frightening, and as we stood back from the searing heat, Brother Laurence and his fire-fighting monks arrived at the scene. To their credit, they had responded with remarkable speed, and were completely professional in their approach, but the fire had gained a firm hold. They managed to save part of the floor, and a couple of nesting boxes. The rest was burnt to the ground.

'Sorry, Arthur,' apologised Brother Laurence unnecessarily. 'We couldn't do a thing.'

'Nobody could have done more,' Arthur sounded dejected, but he spoke the truth. 'It was all Sam's fault!'

'My fault?' cried Sam. 'I didn't light a pipe and lay it in that grass!'

'What's this about a pipe?' I asked, and it was then that the story came out. Brother Laurence chuckled over the yarn, and said he'd found the exercise extremely valuable for his team; real fires, produced in real places under real circumstances, were far better for his men than those created artificially for training. He thanked Arthur for his fire, retrieved all his equipment and drove away through the little gathering of spectators.

My next duty was to complete a Fire Report, and I decided to write this one off as 'Accidental – No suspicious circumstances', for I dare not include the fact that Arthur had deliberately laid his glowing pipe in the grass to see if it would destroy the henhouse. That could raise all kinds of questions from Sergeant Blaketon, so I simply wrote that hot ash had accidentally fallen from his pipe into the grass, and

162

the wind had fanned it into a blaze which had swept towards the tinder-dry henhouse. The value was about £25, as near as I can remember, and no lives were lost. The hens were without shelter for several days afterwards, and laid their eggs all over the place, but the incident provided Aidensfield with a lovely talking point.

It would be eight or nine weeks later when I popped into the Brewers Arms and saw the irascible pair at a window table.

'That fire wae all your fault, Sam,' Arthur was saying. 'If you'd never doubted me, it would never have happened.'

'Doubted you? What do you mean? You did the first one with your pipe, and you did the second in exactly the same way! What's it got to do with doubting?'

'Friends aren't supposed to doubt each other,' Arthur was saying. 'If you'd believed my word, I wouldn't have lit that pipe and put it where it could fall over ...'

'Arthur, you old sod, you set fire to your own henhouse and it's no good blaming anybody else.'

'When that grass grows again,' he said, 'I'll show you...'

'Then we'd better get Brother Laurence standing by right from the start!' laughed Sam. 'It might be your own house that goes up in smoke next time!'

'My house is too well built for that sort of fire to catch hold!' said Arthur.

'It's not!' argued Sam. 'Fires can burn stones and bricks,' and I left before they could dream up any more of their dangerous schemes.

Police Constable Michael Sealifant transferred to the Eltering Sub-Division of the North Riding Constabulary from Birmingham City Police because he was sick of urban grime and suburban attitudes. He wanted to find himself, to be close to nature, and to live in a countryside free from pollution and the threat of the atomic bomb.

In those days, the transfer of individuals between police forces was fairly common, especially at constable rank, but if higher ranks wished to transfer to fill a vacancy in a new force, there was opposition on the grounds that the incoming man of rank was denying a local man promotion.

But when constables made application, they were favourably looked upon because there was always a shortage of men, especially those with experience, and it was felt that officers with police experience in other areas could bring untold benefits to our small force.

And so it was with Police Constable Michael Sealifant, aged 29, married with two children. His parent force wrote a glowing account of this man and his potential, but such reports are always regarded with suspicion on the grounds that if he was so good, why did they want to release him? When someone writes a glowing report about a man wishing to leave, it is usually done to make sure he goes. Even so, we accepted P.C. Michael Sealifant into our bosom, and the Chief Constable allocated him a rural beat house near Eltering. It was in a village called Fellerthorpe, which lies on the edge of the moors and is graced by wide open spaces, moorland sheep, summer visitors and winter tempests.

Because of its remoteness, no one in the North Riding Force wanted the beat, and so the house had remained empty for seven or eight years. But young Mike, in his desire for rural bliss, reckoned this was the answer to all his dreams. He looked at the house, liked it, and said he would accept the posting.

For the Chief Constable, it represented an additional

man, albeit in a very remote area; the beat had remained vacant for all those years simply because it was more important to have officers where there were people who might need them, and not wasting away in the hills. Because Fellerthorpe beat was so remote and unwanted, the Standing Joint Committee had threatened to sell the police house, and this would mean more acres to be supervised by fewer men. The Chief Constable was naturally opposed to this, and because other officers declined the post for domestic reasons (and no one blamed them), P.C. Michael Sealifant was the answer to a Chief Constable's prayer. It was Ben Jonson who talked of 'Service of some virtuous gentleman', and here was a virtuous gentleman who wished to be of service.

On the day of P.C. Sealifant's arrival in Yorkshire, I was on duty. The section at Ashfordly was, for once in its lifetime, fully staffed, which meant I was given a motorcycle patrol which embraced most of the sub-division. That area embraced portions of the Eltering Sub-Division which included Fellerthorpe beat. As was the custom in those halcyon days when a new constable arrived, one of the local men would be allocated to him to help unpack his belongings and generally settle him in. I was therefore told to report to the Police House in remotest Fellerthorpe, there to help the new constable unpack his furniture.

Mike was a real live wire. He was as jumpy as the proverbial nit, always rushing into things and he wanted the pantechnicon unpacked even before its wheels had stopped turning. I introduced myself when he paused for breath, and he said I could help with the heavy stuff, like wardrobes, the settee, his beds and so forth.

He was a very tall, thin individual with a gaunt face and a sallow complexion, topped by a thin thatch of straw coloured hair. His long, slender arms operated rather like windmills, and he continually badgered the removal men to be careful with his crockery, or not to paddle on the bare floorboards. His wife, on the other hand, was a mousey girl who was rather plump, but very nice and open. She brewed copious quantities of tea for us, and managed to rustle up a meal as darkness descended around half past five. It was eggs, chips and peas, and it was gorgeous.

Mick managed to halt himself for this break, and beamed at us all.

'By Jove,' he grinned, his lean cheeks crinkling to show his good teeth, 'this is the life. Look at those moors out there! Listen to the silence … and all that space for the children to play …'

He went into raptures about the location of his new beat, and in some ways he was right. The house, a stone-built cottage-style structure of the last century, was not a standard police house, and possessed great charm and character. It was spacious, which might cause worries over heating it in winter, and it was very isolated. But Mike and his lovely wife, Angie, seemed totally content. Both were looking forward to their life in rural Yorkshire.

I remained with them after the pantechnicon had departed, and helped them unpack much of the smaller stuff, assisting Mike to position things about the house while Angie bathed the two little boys. By nine o'clock that night, it looked more like home, and the blazing coal fire added a cheery dimension to the house. Showing considerable good nature, the inspector at Eltering had dispatched a man over to Fellerthorpe every day for the previous two weeks to light fires in the house, so that it would be aired and cosy for the new arrivals. It was a nice thought, and I know Mike appreciated it.

I took my leave at half past nine. With Mike and Angie at my side, I stood on the front doorstep and we all admired the tremendous views from his porch. In spite of the darkness, we could see the outline of the valley and the dotted lights of houses and villages below were like glow-worms.

'God!' he shouted suddenly. 'What's that?'

His long arm pointed excitedly to a huge blaze somewhere in the valley and a similar one over to the east.

I laughed gently. 'Burning straw,' I informed him. 'When the harvest is in, modern machines leave lots of waste straw behind. It's literally left in long rows in the cornfields and because recovery is so expensive and difficult, the farmers simply set fire to it. It's an easy way to destroy it.'

'There's another one!' and Angie pointed across to the west, where a smaller fire flickered in the darkness.

'You'll see a lot of those this autumn,' I said. 'Don't worry, they're all under control and they're just one of the features of the countryside.'

'I've a lot to learn about the countryside,' he said fiercely, 'but we're going to learn, aren't we, darling?' and he put his arm around his wife's ample waist. I left them standing at the door as they admired the glorious views from their lofty and lonely home.

As I rode away on my Francis Barnett, I wondered how this couple would cope. Living in exotic, remote locations is not easy, especially in the winter, and winter was not many weeks away. It takes a hardened countryman to live without neighbours, shops and the other comforts of civilisation, and yet this man of Birmingham and his wife seemed determined to give it a try. I gave them credit for their determination.

In addition, the house had not been lived in for years, and it was in need of maintenance. Although the fabric was sound, the exterior needed some paint before another winter and I knew the Police Authority would approve the work. They would probably decorate the interior too – the Chief Constable would exercise all his powers of persuasion and charm to effect these considerations for his new, isolated-beat constable.

Another problem was the garden. Its years of neglect had turned it into a veritable hayfield. Long, tough couch grass had rampaged across the garden to conceal paths, rockeries and agricultural patches alike. It had been joined by many other prolific grasses and weeds, making the garden into a tough, thick wilderness. It would need a completely new start.

I didn't envy Mike in his dream house.

Three days later, just after lunch, Sergeant Blaketon called me into his office, and he seemed very fierce when he rang me. It sounded as if I was in trouble.

I drove down to Ashfordly, parked the machine, obeyed all the rules of parking and knocked on his door. My heart was thumping.

'Come in,' came his loud, angry voice.

'Good morning, Sergeant.' I knew that the tone of his voice demanded the utmost respect from me, but I did not know what I had done to aggravate him.

'Rhea,' he said very slowly, 'what in the name of God did you tell that new man?'

'New man?' I spoke stupidly because I had not the remotest idea what he was leading up to.

'The chap with the funny name who's just come to Fellerthorpe.'

'P.C. Sealifant,' I said.

'Yes, what did you tell him?'

'Well.' I was flannelling because I did not know the drift of his questioning. What on earth had the fellow done? Got lost? Gone out to work without telling the Sub-Division? Fallen off his motorbike?

'Go on, Rhea.' Blaketon's voice was ominous.

'Just ordinary things about his work in the countryside,' I tried to sound confident. 'How to meet people, what the folks up here are like, what they expect of police officers, how to check a stock register and renew a firearm certificate ...'

'Go on, Rhea,' he ordered me.

'Well, Sergeant, I can't remember precise things. I mean, there's not a lot you can say when you're humping heavy furniture about.'

'What about straw-burning?' His dark eyes bored into me.

'Straw-burning?' This remark baffled me.

'Yes, Rhea, what did you tell him about straw-burning? That is what I asked.'

'Nothing,' I said, and then I remembered our final conversation on the doorstep. 'Oh,' I halted, then continued, 'just before I left him, he spotted several fires in the valley, around Eltering mainly. He thought something was on fire, so I explained what was happening.'

'Ah, so you did tell him about straw-burning?' He sounded triumphant.

'I only put him right about it, Sergeant. I explained what the farmers were doing with their waste straw.'

'You did, eh? Precisely what did you explain to him?'

'Just that when the harvest is gathered in, the modern machinery leaves behind a lot of waste straw. For economical reasons, and practical reasons, it is disposed of by fire.'

'That's all?'

'Yes, Sergeant.'

'Did you, or did you not, explain the technical ways of actually setting fire to the straw?'

'No,' I almost shouted, still wondering what had happened.

He slumped back in his chair and scowled at me from beneath those heavy black eyebrows.

'Rhea,' he said in a voice loaded with resignation, 'that new man's a bloody liability.' It wasn't often Sergeant Blaketon swore.

'Why?' I had to ask the question and did so hoping it would lead to some form of clarification.

'You know that confounded garden of his, at Fellerthorpe?'

I nodded and recalled the profuse growth of waste grass and weeds.

'He decided the best way to clear his garden was to set fire to it, just like the farmers did with their straw.'

I felt like laughing, and did not know what to say.

Sergeant Blaketon continued, and I could see the beginnings of tears of mirth in his eyes, accompanied by the start of a wide smile on the corners of his mouth. 'Rhea, that bloody man did just that. But do you know how he got it going? He poured *petrol* on the grass and down the path ... petrol! And then he threw a match into it.'

'Sergeant! You're joking ...!' I found myself laughing and he was roaring with laughter too, tears running down his face.

'I'm not joking, Rhea! I wish I was. He had saturated his garden with petrol ... I mean ... the whole lot went up like an explosion ... whoosh ... all on fire ...' He was holding his sides now, and laughing until it hurt. 'Door frame, door, kitchen window ... the stuff had dribbled out of his can, you see ... from the house ... all the kitchen's gone ... he's lost his hair, eyebrows and most of his clothes ... what a bloody mess, Rhea ... what a bloody mess ... the kitchen's gutted ...'

'Is he hurt?' I managed to ask.

'Not a bit. Scared yes, but hurt – no. We're having to rehouse him and his family. They're sending him to South Bank.'

I knew South Bank. In those days, it was in the North Riding, although on a heavy industrial suburb of Middlesbrough, and was known for its grime and tough people. Rather like Birmingham, I suppose.

'He won't have learned much about the countryside, Sergeant,' I said.

'I reckon he's learned quite a bit, Rhea,' he chuckled to himself, wiping the tears from his eyes. 'He'll be able to tell 'em all about straw-burning when he gets to South Bank. He might even become their straw-burning spokesman! I'm sure they burn a lot of straw in South Bank.'

And I left him to his thoughts.

Chapter 8

'Experience teaches slowly, and at the cost of mistakes.'
JAMES ANTHONY FROUDE (1818–94)

ONE BRANCH OF THE police service which has almost slipped into oblivion since World War II is the Special Constabulary. The sturdy folk who join are a supportive arm of the regular Police Force, yet they are ordinary citizens; they rise to the occasion in times of strife and social unrest.

The Specials have a long and interesting history, but came into their own around 1831, the date of the first statute to concern itself specifically with them. In the last century, Specials were used by magistrates during many historic upheavals, such as the Chartist riots, the Rebecca riots, the bread riots, strikes and other type of industrial unrest. As the newly formed regular police forces established themselves, however, the use of Specials declined for this kind of work.

Specials were marvellous as supporters of the police during the two World Wars, and afterwards their role changed. They were not called upon only in times of tumult, but were welcomed as patrolling officers in uniform, when they supplemented the slender blue line by helping out at all kinds of busy times. Examples of their work include first-division football matches, holiday times at the seaside, Saturday night revels, visits by V.I.P.s and the local police station's annual Christmas dinner. When every regular officer wanted to be off duty at the same time, the Specials would take over the town and patrol in their dark-blue uniforms with such efficiency and smartness that few members of the public realised they were not regular officers.

By 1965, their appointment and qualifications were set down in a Statutory Instrument known as the Special Constables Regulations, 1965, which stated that a Special Constable should be not less than eighteen years old, should be of good character and health, and be of British Nationality. There were no height stipulations, although local Chief Constables could determine the height of their own Specials. Few of them accepted men or women who were less than 5 feet 6 inches tall.

A formal training programme was established, with a career structure and pensions for those injured on duty. Specials, however, do not receive payment for their work, although expenses can be approved.

As a consequence, many people with a sense of social duty or vocation, have over the years joined the Specials and have performed useful and dedicated service. To call them hobby bobbies is perhaps unjust, for lots of them serve faithfully as volunteers in other organisations and seem to get themselves involved in almost anything that happens in the community.

Such a man was Maurice Merryman, the undertaker at Ashfordly. He did not fit the usual image of an undertaker, because he was not tall and gaunt, he did not wear black clothes all day and his eyes were not set in deep, shadowy recesses within a skull-like cranium. Instead, Maurice was short and tubby, with a round, pink face and chubby cheeks. His pale grey eyes beamed from behind thick-lensed spectacles, and he wore very smart suits in all his enterprises, although he did wear black for funerals.

Apart from being the undertaker at Ashfordly, he drove the local taxi, sold flowers from a market stall, and ran a fruit shop. He was always busy, always cheerful and constantly available to perform a good turn. Maurice was kindness itself, and that is the reason he became an undertaker. He couldn't bear to think of people being left unburied in cold weather, so he established himself as the local burial expert with a boast that he saw them to their eternal rest in the nicest possible way.

I think he became a Special for similar reasons. He felt that the law could be enforced in a humane way and even believed there was some good in most villains, a belief not shared by the majority of police officers. But Maurice was undeterred by the misgivings of others and set about patrolling the streets of Ashfordly for his stipulated two hours a month. He saw himself there to enforce the law and to do good to the community.

One of his spells of duty occurred during the section dinner. This is one evening out of the whole year when every member of Ashfordly section, including wives and/or girlfriends, is off duty. They go to a local hotel for a good meal and a dance, and it is a social gathering where everyone can meet everyone else. But as the town cannot be left without a police presence, Maurice comes forward on this auspicious night and volunteers for duty. He does more than his required two hours, and happily patrols the streets and supervises the office until normal service is resumed.

One Friday night, therefore, he was performing this duty in our absence and was enjoying a spell in the office where he had made a cup of tea and was reading police circulars. For Maurice, life was good, and he felt very important because during that evening, the law enforcement of Ashfordly lay in his carefully manicured hands.

Around ten o'clock, as he sank his third cup of tea, a car pulled up outside Ashfordly Police Station. It generated more than the usual amount of noise, it braked with some difficulty and parked in what some officers might describe as a haphazard manner. The driver's door slammed as the horn blew accidentally and the lights flickered in unison.

Maurice pricked up his ears and wondered what was to befall him. The metal gate, which led down the police station path, squeaked then clanged against its support, and there followed the shuffling steps of someone heading erratically for the door. Maurice put down his papers and stood behind the counter, waiting.

The heavy door crashed open and in staggered a rounded gentleman. He was enveloped in a cloud of whisky fumes and hiccupped many times as he staggered towards the supportive woodwork of the counter.

'Evening, Officer.' Powerful alcoholic odours enveloped Maurice and his customer as the fellow clung for support. 'Not a bad evening, is it?'

Maurice recognised him as Aubrey Barraclough, a haulage contractor from Brantsford, a man involved in big business and many associated interests. Clearly, the fellow had not recognised Maurice in his blue suit with the shiny buttons; had Maurice been behind the counter of his fruit shop, there would have been instant recognition.

'Hello, Mr Barraclough,' smiled the helpful Special Constable. 'What can we do for you?'

'Oh, it's not the policeman, it's Maurice! I didn't know you'd joined the Force, Maurice?' and he hiccupped.

'I haven't, I'm a Special Constable,' beamed Maurice. 'But tonight, I'm manning the station and looking after things. So what can I do for you?'

'I've come to give myself up,' stated Mr Barraclough. 'I have drunk far too much and feel I cannot be allowed to drive home.'

'Oh,' said Maurice, wondering what he should do with the fellow. 'I'm not sure of the procedures.'

'Well, I will walk home. I am too drunk to drive …'

'No,' said Maurice, 'I cannot allow that. If you leave your car outside, and I let you go, then I will be asked awkward questions. I will be asked why I didn't proceed against you, and that could result in you losing your driving licence. I would have to find a doctor to examine you to determine whether you are fit to drive, and there are all sorts of complications. I cannot let you walk home and leave the car.'

'You are the officer in charge of law enforcement, Maurice, so what do you suggest?' Barraclough swayed rather violently and clutched at the counter to maintain his upright stance.

'If you leave the car outside, I will have to formalise things by arresting and charging you. That'll mean a night in the cells, and a court appearance tomorrow, with lots of publicity for you.'

Barraclough shook his head, an action which made him spin rather like a waltzing top which was losing its momentum.

'No, I just wanted to leave the car, that's all.'

'Well,' said Maurice in his kindest mood. 'You drove it here and you are aware of your condition. You talk lucidly, and you are coherent. I believe you are not too drunk to drive it home, Mr Barraclough, so I suggest you go back to the car and drive home slowly.'

'You do?'

'Yes, I do. That would solve all your problems.'

'You really think so, Maurice? You are a very good policeman, Maurice, a very good one. Yes, all right.'

And Barraclough turned and made for the door. He achieved some success and emerged into the fresh air, whereupon he headed, with a little swaying of the legs and much more hiccupping, towards his waiting car.

No professional police officer would have allowed that to happen, but Maurice was a helpful, kind-hearted undertaker with a penchant for wearing police uniform, and he did not appreciate the problems he thus created.

With a monstrous crashing of gears and a blaring horn, Aubrey Barraclough launched his Daimler upon the town of Ashfordly. Being late at night, (and ten o'clock is late in those peaceful places), the streets were quiet, which was fortunate, because Barraclough's Daimler performed what can only be described as terpsichorean movements along the highways and byways of Ashfordly. The lovely car waltzed and screeched around corners as it made for the Market Place with the intention of taking the road to Brantsford.

Its meandering journey could not hope to end in success, and one of its prime reasons for failure was a keep-left bollard at the junction with the Market Place and the road to Brantsford. When driving along the wide road past the Market Place, Barraclough had noticed the illuminated sign and recognised it as the beginnings of his final run home. He therefore accelerated.

His beautiful car collided magnificently with the bollard, and crumpled to a halt. This threw him forward into the windscreen and caused the bonnet to burst open like the mouth of a gigantic hippopotamus. It is said that

177

Barraclough hiccupped twice, put the car into reverse and dragged it clear. He stepped outside, slammed the bonnet shut and set off in his intended direction.

After travelling only five hundred yards, he collided with a stationary Morris Minor which was parked harmlessly outside a cottage on the outskirts of Ashfordly, and this time his efforts were spectacularly successful. The Morris, just home after a trip to Malton, was lovely and warm, and when Barraclough's speeding Daimler rammed into it, the petrol tank split wide open and the Morris burst into flames. In a very short time, those flames also licked the thwarted Daimler and within minutes, both cars were wildly ablaze. The surrounding houses flickered in the light, and the heat made the road surface bubble as the tar melted.

Barraclough managed to scramble clear and ran for his life, while the owner of the Morris, just tucking into an apple-pie supper, rushed out to see his pride and joy in an advanced state of incineration. He dashed next door to call the fire brigade and the police, while the distant darkness concealed the unsteady departure of Aubrey Barraclough.

Because the fire brigade at Ashfordly comprised part-timers who were now in the pubs, and as the only police presence was Maurice, it took some time to gather wits and equipment. Eventually, these emergency services arrived at the scene.

By the time they did arrive, the Morris was burnt to a cinder and the Daimler had all the appearances of a cast-off shell. Only its number plates were identifiable, so Maurice stated he knew the culprit.

'It's Aubrey Barraclough!' he cried, and promptly began searching the remains of the car for the remains of Mr Barraclough, doubtless with some kind of commercial motive at the back of his mind. But no Aubrey or part of Aubrey was found.

'He'll have run for it!' snarled the owner of the Morris ashes. 'He'll want to avoid being done for drunken driving. He's always drunk ... it's time the bloody police did something about him.'

'I'll make a report about it,' suggested Maurice, not really knowing what he was supposed to do next.

The cunning Aubrey had stumbled down one of the alleys between the cottages, and had found a pedal cycle. Hearing the commotion in his wake, he had jumped on to the cycle with enough sense not to switch on the lights, and with an almost silent swishing of tyres had begun his escape run. By now, he was slightly more sober than hitherto, and knew how to keep his balance; he also knew which way to turn the pedals and the handlebars. As more officials and onlookers began to gather at the scene of the blaze, the dark figure of Aubrey Barraclough, on someone's stolen cycle, moved quietly along the dark road, homeward bound. He could always claim somebody had stolen his Daimler ...

As he began to craftily calculate the best way of extricating himself from any responsibility for the destruction he had left behind, he felt the soothing wind in his hair and the coolness of night upon his cheeks. His podgy legs pressed the pedals and caused his breath to become heavier and more rapid as time progressed. It wasn't long before he actually began to enjoy this sobering-up exercise; he experienced the exhilaration of youth as the cycle sped along its way.

Those of you who know the road from Ashfordly to Brantsford will recall that it weaves through the countryside in a most interesting manner. Some two miles out of Ashfordly, it dips quite suddenly as the highway races down a slope to cross a stream, and at the crossing place, the road turns quite suddenly to the left, before rising to continue its picturesque way.

In a car, that point can be dangerous, but local people such as Aubrey are familiar with this place; they always cope with it, even when slightly intoxicated.

But Aubrey was more than slightly intoxicated; furthermore, he was not in his Daimler with its wonderful brakes and high-quality headlights. Without any headlights to guide him, he hadn't realised he'd come to this point. He reached the summit aboard a pedal cycle of unknown quality, in darkness, and he was singing blissfully to the stars as he pedalled along.

Almost without warning, Aubrey began to gather speed as the cycle started its descent, and it was quite apparent that the bike was going faster than Aubrey wished. He used the brakes, but they were not as efficient as those of his Daimler, especially when carrying seventeen stones, so the cycle refused to reduce its onward pace.

Very soon it was bouncing along at Daimler pace, and Aubrey took his feet off the pedals. He began to wobble; he began to shout for help, but none was forthcoming. By all accounts, his onward path took him across the grass verge at the bottom of the slope, and the cycle collided with the off-side parapet of the bridge.

The cycle stopped but Aubrey did not. We are told that he became airborne for a short distance before the cold waters of Ashford Gill cushioned his heavy return to earth. There must have been an almighty splash as Aubrey arrived at this point, and it is a well known fact that cold water in abundance has a wonderful ability to aid the sobering-up of most drunks.

It is believed that this water did help to sober up

Aubrey, because the abandoned and buckled cycle led to his discovery on the banks of the stream. He was found lying there with his huge belly in the air, all damp and cold, and he was fast asleep. When he was roused, he was very, very sober, and promptly denied everything.

But scientific evidence and eye-witness accounts are marvellous, and within two months Aubrey appeared before Eltering Magistrates' Court. He was charged, among other things, with dangerous driving, malicious damage, failing to report an accident, larceny of a pedal cycle and riding a bike without lights.

For poor Special Constable Merryman, there was the inevitable blasting from the mouth of Sergeant Blaketon, and the unenviable thrill of becoming an object lesson in all future lectures and training sessions, for both specials and regular officers. The Merryman Incident, as it became known, was a lesson in how not to deal with drunken drivers.

But Maurice was retained because of his value on our Section dinner night. We all benefited from his special brand of policemanship.

It was Alexander Pope who produced those famous words 'To err is human', but lots of us forget the words which follow, for they are 'to forgive, divine'.

If the police officers of Ashfordly learned anything from Special Constable Merryman's mistakes, it was that mistakes can occur even if the intention is honourable. Poor Maurice Merryman's intentions were always honourable, and with that knowledge in mind, I found myself wanting to assist the less fortunate. Police officers are constantly meeting those who need help and guidance, and lots of unofficial and unpublicised assistance is given by them. But could such help ever be wrong? Could there be a time when help from a police officer was a mistake? I was not afraid of making a mistake, for mistakes happen to everyone, but could I forgive or be forgiven if I did?

The opportunity to find out came on Sunday morning when I was off duty. I was cutting the lawn outside the front of my hilltop police house when Gordon Murray came to the gate.

Gordon was a young man of twenty-eight who worked as a labourer on building sites. Stocky, with brooding dark eyes and a thick head of wavy hair, he was a good-looking man whose burly figure and cavalier approach to life attracted a lot of women. He had had many girl friends, who fluttered to him like moths to a bright light, but he had never succumbed to marriage.

I had known him a while; he ran an old van which was always falling foul of the law because of its condition or its lack of tax and insurance. Another of his foibles was to fight everyone in sight after he had enjoyed four or five pints of beer. Sometimes sullen and moody, he was strong and fit, and a good worker when he felt like it. He could also be a thorough troublemaker when the mood took him — he was certainly unpredictable.

During my short time at Aidensfield, I'd had several confrontations with him, many when he was fighting fit on a Saturday night, and fortunately I managed to cool his earthy antagonism; he was good enough to respect the uniform I wore, and sensible enough to take my regular advice to 'get away home before there's any more trouble'. Without me there, he would speedily launch himself into any situation, good or bad, and at times would emerge with black eyes, bruised groin and flattened nose. Sometimes he was the victor, sometimes the vanquished.

182

Even though I had taken him to court for many motoring offences, and dragged him off umpteen opponents outside dance halls and pubs, there was a peculiar kind of respect and friendship between us. In his sober, upright moods, he would do anything for me; he once saved me from a beating up when some thugs came from Stokesley to do battle with the Ashfordly youths. In return, I always assured him that if he needed the kind of help I could give, he should not be afraid to ask.

And so here he was, standing at my garden gate one Sunday morning. He was casually dressed in a rough shirt and jeans, and his muscular arms were bronzed and firm after working out of doors for so long. He pushed open the gate and approached me. He looked rather nervous, for he was well out of his territory; visiting police establishments voluntarily was not in keeping with his character.

'Hello, Mr Rhea.' He always referred to me in this way, never by my Christian name.

'Hello, Gordon,' I greeted him. 'This is an honour – do you fancy a coffee?'

'Er, well,' this meant he must enter the awesome portals of the police house, but he accepted and followed me into the lounge. I took him there because I was off duty, and because I felt he'd come for reasons which were not official. Mary produced two cups of coffee and closed the door as Gordon sweated over the purpose of his visit.

'Now, Gordon, what's troubling you?'

He played with the cup of coffee, moving it nervously in his heavy hands. He kept his eyes averted from me as he tussled with his problem.

I waited; I had seen this kind of hesitancy before and knew that any prompting from me might cause him to dry up entirely; whatever was on Gordon's mind must be important because it was most unlike him to enter a police house or to make an initial approach of this kind. But I had him cornered – he was not outside a pub where he could walk off; he was on my settee, in my lounge, with a cup of my coffee in his hands.

I sipped my coffee, waiting, and then he looked at me earnestly.

'Mr Rhea,' he began, 'you might have heard about me …'

He paused, as if expecting a reply, but I did not know what to say.

'You mean something recent?' I put to him.

'Aye. About me getting married,' he blushed vividly.

'Married?' I cried. 'No, Gordon, that's news to me. Well, is it true?'

He nodded and a shy smile flitted across his features. 'Aye,' he said, 'It's right enough. That's why I've come to see you.'

'Go on,' I inched forward in my seat. 'First, though, congratulations. I think you'll enjoy married life.'

'Aye, well, it's summat I'm not used to, being settled. I've allus gone where I've pleased. I mean, my old mum looks after me, washes my clothes and does my food and things … and there's all sorts I don't know …'

'About the ceremony you mean?'

'That as well. But everything. Flowers and the church, all that.'

'The vicar will help you with the formalities,' I advised him. 'In fact, I think he's got a little book that tells you step by step how to organise everything from the organist to the reception, even the honeymoon.'

'I've him to see next,' he said. 'Me, seeing a vicar!' and he raised his eyes as if to Heaven.

'Mr Clifton will make sure things are running smoothly,' I assured him. 'Is this why you wanted to see me?'

He nodded, and took a long drink from the mug of coffee, then wiped his mouth with the back of his hand.

'Aye,' he said, 'Well, I've done a bit of asking about, to try and find out what I'm to do, and …'

He paused again, took another long drink as I awaited his next worry. He was approaching another difficult speech.

'Go on, Gordon,' I tried to ease the problem out of him.

'Well, they say the most important bloke at a wedding is the best man. He's got to make sure things go right, hasn't he? Get the bride to the altar, fix the reception and things. You know, jolly things along, and keep things right, make speeches and all that.'

'Yes, that's true, Gordon. Most men, when they are thinking of getting married, make sure they choose a good best man for that reason. He's got all sorts of jobs to see to – he keeps the wedding running smoothly. Yes, you need a good best man.'

'Well,' he licked his lips. 'That's why I'm asking you.'

At first, his words did not mean a lot; I thought he was asking me for my advice, but it gradually dawned that he was asking *me* to be his best man.

'Me?' I cried. 'You're asking me to be your best man, Gordon?'

'Aye, well, none of my mates are up to it, and I've no brothers and no dad, and I do want things to go right and real smooth …'

'Who's the lucky girl, then?' I had to know this before committing myself.

'Sharon Pollard, she works over at Thirsk in one of the hotels. Lives in.'

I shook my head. 'I don't know her, Gordon. Where's the wedding to be?'

'In Aidensfield,' he said.

'Not Thirsk?'

'No, she's not a local. She's from Liverpool, just working here, and doesn't want to go back there. So she'll live in our house, as a lodger, before the wedding.'

'Well,' I said, 'this is a turn-up for the books, Gordon! You're the last man I expected to see going to the altar. She must be a real cracker to have caught you.'

I paused, and I knew he was awaiting my answer. I knew his earthy background, and his equally earthy relations, most of whom were petty villains of one kind or another. He was from a noted family of local villains. What they would think to a policeman being best man at Gordon's wedding was something I could never guess, but he had asked me as a friend. In some ways, I was very flattered, if a little puzzled by his odd request.

'All right,' I smiled, realising it must have been a difficult request for him to make, 'I'll do it. Gordon, it will be a pleasure. I will be proud to be your best man.'

His face lit up and he leaned across to shake hands with me.

'Mr Rhea,' he said, 'this has made me a very happy man.'

After he'd gone, I told Mary the news.

'You've what?' she gasped.

'I've agreed to be best man for Gordon Murray,' I repeated.

'Why?' she demanded.

'Because he asked me,' I answered. 'He came specially to ask me, and I agreed. I think it's a great

186

honour.'

'You must be stupid!' she said flatly. 'If a man like that asks a policeman to be best man, you can bet there'll be a catch in it.'

'I owe him a favour,' I tried to justify my actions. 'He says none of his relations or friends is capable ...'

'They'll all be drunk, that's why,' she said. 'You should hear the gossip about the Murrays in the shop. They're a right lot – there's that cousin of his who's a scrap-dealer and always in court for stealing, there's that other cousin from Eltering who got fined for dealing in drugs, and another who steals cars ... Nicholas, what have you let yourself in for?'

'I am going to be best man at the wedding of a friend!' I said, 'and that's final.'

I must admit that Mary's misgivings had given me cause for concern, and it was probably wise to keep this assignment from the eyes and ears of Sergeant Blaketon and the other officers at Ashfordly. Later, when Gordon confirmed the date and time of his wedding, I applied for a day's leave and it was approved. Over the weeks that followed, Gordon came to the house a good deal, and he accepted his new responsibilities with remarkable aplomb. I liked him in these moods; he was affable, courteous and very anxious that his wedding day would be a success.

Mary grew to like him too, for she kept us supplied with coffee, and when the official invitation came, she was included as a guest. Gordon readily accepted the practices governing the bride's parents, her family and guests, and those of the groom, and I could see he was genuinely looking forward to his new state of matrimony.

Some six weeks before the May wedding, Sharon arrived at his mother's house, and Gordon brought her to the police house to meet us. She was a pretty girl, extraordinarily thin with long black dull hair and a pale smooth face. She had the slender figure of a model, and the unmistakable accent of a Liverpudlian. Her clothes were on the dowdy side, her shoes down at heel and her fingernails black with dirt. But Gordon loved her.

Mary brewed the inevitable coffee, and Sharon played with our children as we made small talk about weddings, bridesmaids, honeymoons, and that sort of thing. Sharon did not talk about her background, other than to tell us her father was dead, and there were seven of them in her family, she being the youngest. She had come over to Thirsk for work, because there was so little in Liverpool; the Thirsk job had come to her notice through one of her father's old Army friends.

I was pleased to meet Gordon's chosen bride, and when they'd gone, Mary said, 'She's pregnant.'

'Never!' I chided her. 'She's too thin …'

'She is pregnant, Nicholas,' Mary affirmed. 'I can tell – any woman can tell. It's the skin and the eyes … Gordon's going to be a dad, and this is obviously a rushed job. She's nice, though, isn't she, even if she's a bit scruffy.'

'She'll be good for Gordon.' I believed that to be true. 'He was telling me they've been allocated an estate cottage at Briggsby, so that'll get him from under his mother's feet.'

As the weeks passed, I began to appreciate that Mary's diagnosis had been correct. Sharon did look a little more plump around the waistline, but it was not a plumpness which would be noticed by a casual observer. I did not hear any other hints of her condition during my patrolling, nor did I seek any clarification on that point. The fact was that Gordon loved her, which he told me several times, and it was evident that Sharon loved him. I believed it would be a fine match, if a little volatile at times.

On the night before the wedding, Sharon's mother and two of her little nieces arrived in Aidensfield and were accommodated in a holiday cottage, rented for the weekend. There was no room and I turned to see it was Sharon's mother. She was holding a handkerchief to her face as the tears cascaded down her plump cheeks. Apart from this, the church was silent as the Rev. Roger Clifton opened with those famous words, 'Dearly beloved, we are gathered here in the sight of God, and in the face of this congregation, to join together this man and this woman in Holy Matrimony ...'

My part in the ceremony was not over-taxing, but the service and its non-musical, watery accompaniment by Sharon's mum caused the time to pass rapidly and before I knew what was happening, I had handed over the ring, Sharon and Gordon were pronounced man and wife, and everyone was filing outside for the photographs.

There was some boisterous noise and rather physical jockeying for position in the photographs, through which Sharon beamed beautifully and Gordon looked every inch the handsome groom. Being best man, I did a lot of cajoling, pleading and ordering about; I started to fix the line-ups for the cameraman and brushed dust off Gordon's suit. I did a lot of running about, but as the hustle of the photographic session continued, I became vaguely aware of some unrest.

At first, my ears were not attuned to sounds beyond my immediate duties, and I associated the loud voices and frequent shrieks with happiness, euphoria and general high spirits. The truth was that other spirits were at work, such as gin and vodka. Sadly, they were acting upon the ample figure of Sharon's mother, who wanted to be in all the photographs with two fingers raised to the heavens.

At first, her insistence on being in every photograph was something of a chuckle, but when she raised her two fingers in what was definitely not a Victory sign, it was evident she had some kind of chip on her shoulders or a massive grudge of some kind. It dawned on me, as I'm sure it had already dawned on the other family guests, that Mrs Pollard was determined to cause trouble or embarrassment.

The photographer did his best to arrange some pictures without her, but it was becoming impossible; even when he arranged a line-up of bridesmaids, she would hustle in just as he had focused his camera, and dislodge the line by charging at them like a raging bull. If there can be an analogy, she was like a cow in a china shop.

Had I been a policeman on duty and distanced from the soul of the ceremony, I would have recognised the onset of trouble because that would have been part of my work, especially at a wedding with such characters as the chief actors. Because I was best man I was heavily committed with the internal arrangements and was not aware of the simmering brew being brought to the boil by Mrs Pollard. I learned later that she had had two half-bottles of gin in her ample handbag, and had been sipping these in church and afterwards, all the time working herself up to a pitch of antagonism.

When I found myself thinking like a policeman instead of a best man, I sought guidance from Gordon. Having caught his eye, I took him to one side as the harassed photographer tried to arrange a picture of both mothers.

'What's her game, Gordon?'

'Trouble,' he said. 'She is out to cause trouble, the bitch!'

'I can see that, but why?'

'Because I put Sharon up the stick, and because she doesn't like me.'

'She was all right in church,' I said. 'If she had any objections, she could have made her case known before coming here.'

'She did, that's why Sharon left home to live here. Mrs Pollard's a real bitch ... she was supping gin in church, Mr Rhea, to get herself worked up for this.'

'She's going to ruin things for you, and there's the reception to come yet, with wine and more drinks. You don't want that ruined, do you?'

'No,' he said, looking at me steadily. 'She's out to make a mess of my wedding day, Mr Rhea. Sharon said she would.'

'Then we'll have to stop her. Is there a useful heavyweight woman on your side?'

'No, Mr Rhea, that's not the way to do it. Anybody from my side would only stir up her lot to fight back. They'd all join in. You need somebody from her side to sort her out.'

'But they'll be sympathetic to her, won't they? And they're all from Liverpool, aren't they? They won't want Yorkshire folk sorting them out, will they?'

'No, Mr Rhea.'

I could sense the beginnings of embarrassment. All around were roughs and toughs from two warring, insensitive families, and the centre of the problem was the troublesome Mrs Pollard. Even now, she was thrusting herself before the camera with two fingers in the air, and lifting her skirts to reveal long green

191

knickers as she did an awful rendering of the can-can. Her family laughed; Gordon's snarled, while Sharon clung to Gordon, not knowing whether to laugh, cry or fade away somewhere.

Their happiness was rapidly degenerating into something uncontrollable; our peaceful village was about to experience the warlike enjoyment of Liverpool's back streets combined with the skills of some of the toughest scrappies and layabouts in Yorkshire. I was off duty, too, in civilian clothes; I was a real pig in the middle.

I had to do something, not only for my sake, but the sake of Gordon and his bride, and for the village. Then, fortuitously, I caught Mary's eye; she was behind a gathered knot of chortling fools who were encouraging Mrs Pollard to kick her legs higher as the poor photographer tried to get Gordon's family group on file.

I signalled to Mary to move aside, and indicated that I wanted to talk to her. She recognised the concern on my face, and inched away from the ogling crowd.

Where there is a focal point for trouble, one solution is to remove that focal point; on this occasion, it meant neutralising Mrs Pollard in some way. She was the catalyst; she was playing to the audience of Liverpudlian admirers and causing everlasting embarrassment to her unfortunate daughter. Gordon's relations wouldn't stand for much more.

Desperate tactics were needed and as I moved aside to talk with Mary, a dreadful scheme crossed my mind. Even as I reached Mary, Mrs Pollard had kicked the camera's tripod over and was trying to dance with the photographer, as her grinning clan stood around and clapped like natives during a ritual dance. For my plan, Mary was neutral; very few knew who she was.

'Mary,' I whispered as she reached me. 'Go to the pub and ask George to remove every drop of liquor from the reception, quickly. Have a bottle of wine ready for the top table, for the bride and groom, but tell him, from me, that there's going to be trouble if this lot have more to drink. Replace the guests' wine with bottles of tonic water or something non-alcoholic. I'll take the responsibility for that. Tell him also, I think he'd better close his pub before the reception. We don't want this lot getting right in there. Tell him they're likely to wreck his bar for the fun of it.'

'Will he do all that?' she asked.

'Tell him what's going on, then I'm sure he will. Then, while I create a diversion here, ring the office and get a police car to patrol the street. There will be one in the area, it'll be patrolling my beat in my absence. Tell them from me it's important. If there's a double crew, then that will be better. Got it?'

She looked at me slyly and I knew what was going through her mind.

'Best man, eh?' she grinned. 'Gordon's no fool ... now you know why he asked you!'

'Rubbish!' I snorted, and returned to the mêlée as she hurried about her mission. I began my diversion. I took the harassed photographer to one side, and said we needed the bride and groom photographed while shaking hands with each of the guests. I knew this would take a long time, and it might placate some of them; I spoke to Gordon and Sharon who agreed, and so the marathon began. Sharon was viciously cursing her mother who tried to pop up behind the groups, two fingers raised, and the language from the others was boisterous, rude and crude. But this part of the ploy was working.

The buffet could wait while everyone was pictured,

and thanks now to the antics of Mrs Pollard, it was taking a considerable time. This suited me – I needed time. Then I saw Mary pushing through the throng, and she was smiling.

'I've seen George, and he's going to move the drinks out. He thanked you for the warning. He says the waiter will produce a bottle of wine for the groom and bride when it's needed – if it's left on the table somebody will pinch it. He'll close the pub now, he says.'

'Good. Now, did you find a car?'

'Yes, Sergeant Bairstow was in the office when I rang, and he's coming right away.'

'Good. I must talk to him without this lot seeing me. When he comes, look out for him, and ask him to drive into the garage. I'll ring him there from the pub's phone.'

'You're being very devious!' she said, with a worried frown.

'We're dealing with a very volatile and devious bunch,' I said. 'Just look out for the Ashfordly car, please.'

Ten minutes went by; Mrs Pollard took another long swig from a bottle she pulled from her handbag, and she paraded before the admiring Liverpudlians to raucous guffaws and loud hand-clapping. Gordon, I felt, was very patient; his poor little wife spent her time in an embarrassed silence.

Eventually, above the heads of the crowd, I noticed the police car enter the village and glide smoothly along the street. I did not acknowledge it. From the corner of my eye, I saw Mary detach herself from a little mob and talk to Sergeant Bairstow, who then drove onwards and turned on to the garage forecourt. He vanished from view; Mary raised her hand and I recognised the signal.

'I'm just going over to the pub,' I called loudly to Gordon, 'won't be a tick. I want to check the buffet.'

He nodded, but the others who heard my words did not react.

I began to feel a little happier as I tapped on the front door which George had already locked, and he let me in.

'Can I use your phone please, George. It's important.'

'They're a rough bloody lot, Mr Rhea,' he said. 'We don't often see weddings like that here.'

'We don't George. Now, I'm going to prevent trouble – I hope.'

He led me to the telephone and I rang Aidensfield Garage, only a few yards up the street, and asked if Sergeant Bairstow was there. He was, and he was brought to the phone.

'P.C. Rhea,' I announced, 'Good morning, Sergeant.'

'What's all the fuss, Nick?' he laughed. 'I see you've got a right shower here today!'

'It's the bride's mother, a real troublemaker. She's going to stir up something … she's drinking herself into a stupor and it seems she intends wrecking the wedding reception; she'll get the backing of these louts for whatever she does. I fear for the reception. I've moved all the booze away.'

'And you want rid of the old lady?' he anticipated my request.

'Yes.'

'Any ideas?' he asked me.

'She's called Pollard, and she's one of a rough family clan from Liverpool. They're all villains, I reckon, and she's obviously the ring-leader.'

'Go on.'

'I thought about having her arrested for something, like suspicion of being wanted on warrant for nonpayment of a fine, or anything. Conduct likely to cause a breach of the peace even. Just to keep her out of the way until the reception's over, and the bride's left for her honeymoon.'

'Very devious, young Nick, very devious and highly improper!'

'But very practicable and a means of preventing crime,' I retorted. 'If she stays, they'll do something bloody awful. She's out to make the groom suffer.'

'If we go in there, in uniform, to lift her, we'll start a riot!'

'I will bring her here, to the garage. All you do is take her away for a couple of hours.'

'You say this lot are the Pollards from Liverpool?' he said.

'Yes, Sarge.'

'Then they are a right set of villains. Right, Nick, you're on.'

I was surprised he knew of their reputation. I replaced the telephone and returned to the fray. There was more loud singing and bawdy shouting, and I saw Mrs Pollard stagger to one side as someone tried to dance with her in the street. I approached her.

'Mrs Pollard,' I whispered, 'I'm the best man.'

'I seen yer, mister best man ...'

'We've arranged a special picture session for you, in colour,' I whispered. 'As a treat, for the bride's mum. But I don't want the others to know.'

'Colour? Me?' and she lifted her skirts to show off those green pantaloons.

'Sssh!' I hissed. 'Just come with me ...'

She stooped low, as if ducking under low arches, and we crept away from the crowd; someone shouted after her, but she put her finger to her lips and indicated silence. The man withdrew, and I breathed a sigh of relief. The walk to the garage was about a hundred yards, and soon we were out of sight.

'It's a studio down here,' I said, clutching her arm.

I took her into the office of the garage, and there Sergeant Bairstow and P.C. Alwyn Foxton awaited.

'Jessie Pollard?' he asked, and the sight of the uniform sobered her immediately. I was surprised when he used her Christian name.

'Bastards!' she hissed. 'You bastards!'

'Jessie Pollard,' chanted Sergeant Bairstow, 'I am arresting you for failing to answer bail this morning, when you were ordered to appear today at Liverpool Magistrates' Court on a charge of shoplifting ...'

Her reply was unprintable, and she fell to the ground, shouting and swearing, kicking her legs in the air and generally creating a mini-riot all of her own. But Sergeant Bairstow and Alwyn between them were able to cope, and bundled her into the rear seat of the two-door car then sped off in the opposite direction to avoid her family.

I returned to the gathering, and saw that the photographer was having some success. I waited until everyone had been pictured, and then shouted over their heads that it was time to eat.

It is not necessary to recount the progress of the reception, except to say that I stood before the gathering and apologised for the lack of alcohol by saying the hall was a temperance hall. The only alcoholic drinks permitted were those for the bride and groom. There was a lot of muttering and shuffling of feet, but as the reception got under way, the good food kept both sides happy.

I also announced the absence of the bride's mother by

saying we had arranged a surprise for Mrs Pollard, a special photographic session in Malton, and so she could not attend the reception. Actually, it was true, because her photo would be taken in the cells. She might be back to see the departure of the bride and groom, I said, and everyone cheered. George's food was splendid, and the drinks he had supplied seemed to placate the turbulent crowd. The speeches were well received, and by two o'clock, it was time for bride and groom to leave. Two o'clock was also the official closing time for the local pubs, and so another little crisis was averted. The pub was officially shut.

Gordon and his happy bride got away safely and I was pleased. Mrs Pollard's real moment of triumph, whatever it was going to be, had evaporated, and she spent the rest of the day in Malton Police Station awaiting an escort from Liverpool Police. She was not going to miss her court appearance a second time.

Two days later, when I saw Sergeant Bairstow, I said, 'Thanks for coming to the rescue, Sergeant. You saved the day.'

'No; thank you, Nick. That woman *was* wanted for jumping bail in Liverpool. She was Jessie Pollard.'

'Was she?'

'Not long before your wife rang with that weird message, we received a call from Liverpool to say she'd jumped bail. They knew she was attending her daughter's wedding somewhere near Ashfordly, and suggested we knock her off after the wedding. We checked with churches and register offices in the area, and the Aidensfield wedding was the only one. We were going to sit and wait until things were over, then move in and arrest her for Liverpool. She's a right villain, they say.'

'So if she had not jumped bail, you might not have come to my rescue?'

'That's an academic question, Nick old son,' he grinned.

But I wondered how many grooms had commenced their married life by getting their mother-in-law arrested.

Chapter 9

'And they are gone; aye, ages long ago, These lovers
fled away into the storm.'

JOHN KEATS (1795–1821)

IRENE HOOD WAS A shy, bespectacled girl of around
nineteen when I first became aware of her existence. She
was not the prettiest of young ladies but she had a lovely
personality and charming manners, each made more
attractive by her modest behaviour and quiet lifestyle.

Every morning, she would push her red pedal-cycle
down the grassy track beside the large house in
Aidensfield where she lived, and would ride along the
leafy lanes to Maddleskirk Abbey where she worked in
the kitchens. I was never quite sure what her duties were,
but it was something fairly mundane like looking after
the vegetables and laying the tables for the daily turn-
over of 120 meals. This undemanding work kept Irene
content and her meagre earnings enabled her to buy
sufficient clothes for her needs, and helped her to
maintain her bicycle and save a little in the Post Office.

Her mouse-like existence came gradually to my
attention; sometimes when I was on early patrol, I would
park my Francis Barnett near the telephone kiosks either
outside Maddleskirk Abbey or near Aidensfield Post
Office. If I chanced to be at either place between twenty
minutes to eight and ten minutes to eight, I would see

Irene on her polished bicycle heading towards the Abbey.

In winter, she rode with her head down against the fierce winds which drove through the valley, and she wore a khaki-coloured anorak with a hood which concealed her face. On her feet would be sensible rubber boots and thick leggings, so that the figure beneath all this clothing remained rather a mystery.

By the time summer came, the same bicycle bore a young lady with short sandy hair, heavy spectacles and a working smock of dark green which covered sensible dresses and legs which wore thick brown stockings and flat shoes. The face beneath the spectacles was pale and slightly freckled, and she had grey/green eyes, nice sound teeth and, when the mood took her, a pretty smile.

Each working morning therefore she rode this cycle to work and each evening at four-thirty she rode it back to Aidensfield. My regular trips along the lane between the Abbey and Aidensfield made me aware of this girl's journeys, and I mentally logged this information as a piece of my growing store of local happenings, which might or might not one day be of value. At that stage, I did not know the girl's name, or where she lived.

As time went by, I sometimes noticed her pushing her cycle up the grassy path at the side of a long, low house built of brick. At the time this knowledge meant nothing to me, but as the weeks and months passed, I learned that the brick house was owned by a Miss Sadie Breckon, and that the quiet girl was Irene Hood, her niece.

At least, everyone said it was aunt and niece. Some persistent gossip hinted the girl was the natural daughter of Sadie Breckon, and that she had been adopted with a changed name for appearances' sake. Whatever the history of the two women, they kept themselves very much out of village activities, and Miss Sadie's only trips were to the post office for stamps and to the shops for her groceries. Where they bought things which would not be obtained in the village, no one knew, unless they resorted to catalogues for their clothes and furniture.

Sadie Breckon did not have a job, and I do not know how she supported herself; the house was huge and was probably paid for, but there were running expenses, rates and heating plus the day-to-day living costs of the two women it sheltered. Irene's income would barely support her, so I guessed that Sadie must have a private income.

Over the following months, I observed that young Irene had become unhappy. Although it is no part of a village policeman's duties to make unhappy girls happy I was a little concerned; my observations were born of regular sightings of the girl, and of the telling change in her facial appearance. Instead of the open, placid face I associated with my early sightings of Irene, there was now a morose appearance. I hoped it did not herald some unpleasant work for me – young girls with problems were liable to do awful things to themselves, but I felt Irene was too sensible to behave stupidly.

On several occasions, I passed her in the street when I was walking along the footpath. She would pass by with a sad smile, but would never speak unless I bade her 'good morning' or 'good afternoon'. Then she would smile her quick reply before scurrying off, head down, into Aunt Sadie's long brick house. I got the impression of a lonely, unhappy teenager.

I think it is fair to say that these observations were made in passing moments; they were fleeting impressions of a young girl without sex appeal. A mouse. Almost a nonentity. A girl who never mixed, and whose lifestyle behind those brick walls was of no interest to anyone. Probably, I would have forgotten all about Irene had it not been for Andrew Pugh.

Andrew drove the bread-van which called at the Abbey's kitchens every day around eight-thirty; it came from Scarborough on a regular run, and I used to see it entering Aidensfield, where it called at the shop, and then went along the lane towards Maddleskirk Abbey. I never had cause to talk to the driver or to become acquainted with him, and it was some time later that I learned of Andrew's name and job.

It seemed that after Andrew had unloaded a massive daily order of bread, teacakes and buns at the Abbey, he would chat to the shy girl who brewed him a quick coffee. That girl was Irene. From those morning chats there developed a stronger liaison, and it wasn't long before Irene found herself deeply in love.

Andrew, it seems, had also fallen head over heels in love with this shy country lass. She was so refreshingly different from the loud, forceful girls he knew at home, and he became spellbound with her calm face and smiling eyes. But he lived at Scarborough which was an hour's drive from Aidensfield. He did possess a motorcycle, but that was not the solution to his problem. The snag was that Sadie wouldn't let Irene out of the house after work. If Andrew wanted to see her other than during his quick morning coffee break, he had to drive out of Scarborough on a Sunday morning and park in Aidensfield. He knew that Sadie and Irene walked side by side to the little Methodist chapel at 10.30 a.m. and back again at 11.30 a.m. each Sunday morning.

But cups of coffee in a monastery kitchen, and sly casts behind Aunty's back near the chapel railings, are no way to conduct a romance. This was the reason for Irene's misery. There must have been love if Andrew bothered to drive nearly forty miles on a Sunday morning for little more than a glimpse of his beloved in her best clothes.

I am not quite sure when I was made aware of these facts, but they are the kind of information that a village police officer assimilates during his day-to-day contact with the people. I had never been inside Sadie's large brick house, nor had I ever spoken to Aunt Sadie; indeed, other than my formal greetings on the footpath, I had never held a conversation with Irene.

And then, by one of those peculiar flukes of circumstances, two motor-cars collided in Aidensfield village street just as Sadie was heading towards the post office to buy some stamps. She saw everything, and one of the drivers had the foresight to take her name before reporting the accident to the police.

This singular act meant that I had to call upon Aunt Sadie to take a written statement from her. I needed her account of the accident because she was the only independent witness. As I walked up that grass path to the rear door of the long, interesting building, all these little facets of Irene's life registered in my mind.

It was a Tuesday evening when I knocked, a late spring evening with darkness yet to come. The back kitchen door needed a coat of paint; it was black and the old paint was peeling off; following my knock, I heard footsteps and Irene answered.

'Oh, hello,' I said in recognition. 'Is Miss Sadie Breckon in?'

'It's my aunt, I'll bring her,' and she dipped indoors in a trice, vanishing into the dark interior and leaving me on the stone doorstep.

Soon, the lady of the house arrived and smiled at me, albeit with some concern on her face.

'Miss Breckon?' I asked. 'Sadie Breckon?'

'Yes, is it about the accident?'

'It is,' I said. 'I believe you witnessed it.'

'Yes, I did. Come in. It's Mr Rhea, isn't it?'

'Yes, we haven't met,' and I stepped into the dark house, removing my cap as I did so, and then I shook hands with her. She led me through the back porch, where I noticed a stock of coal and Irene's bicycle. We entered an old-fashioned kitchen where there was a Yorkist range with a coal fire blazing cheerily in the grate. The timeless picture was completed by a kettle singing on the range, a floor of flagged sandstones and several clip rugs scattered about the room. It was like stepping back half a century or more, but the place was beautifully warm and snug.

I passed the scrubbed wooden table, stepped down into the next room and found myself in another old-fashioned area. There was an old horsehair settee, lots of rugs and plants about the place, and ancient pictures on the walls, many depicting long-dead ancestors. It was a veritable museum. Irene was standing in front of one of the chairs.

'This is my niece, Irene,' and I smiled at her.

'Yes, we pass each other most mornings, don't we, Irene? I'm pleased to meet you,' and the girl shook my hand delicately, her eyes not meeting mine as she blushed. Her cheeks turned a bright red and she knew this was happening, so she sat down and buried herself in a book.

'She reads a lot,' her aunt said. 'Romances, gothics, that sort of thing, filling her head with all kinds of notions.'

'There's not a lot for a young girl to do in the village,' I sympathised with Irene.

'They can get into trouble anywhere!' snapped the aunt, and I had no idea what lay behind that remark.

Now that we were in the room, as it was termed, she settled me on the horsehair settee and smiled. 'Well, tell me what you want to know, Mr Rhea.'

I reminded her briefly about the circumstances of the collision and she nodded in agreement. 'Yes,' she beamed. 'I saw everything. Such a silly man. I wrote his number down,' and she disappeared into an adjoining room to locate a piece of paper. I looked about the room and smiled at Irene who caught my eye with a shy glance before Aunt Sadie returned flourishing a piece of paper. It was a comparatively simple task to get the statement written down in chronological order, and she was quite happy to add her signature at its conclusion.

That short visit was my first to this strangely old-fashioned home, but it did enable me to speak to the shy girl whom I saw most mornings. Thereafter when she passed, she would hold her head high and smile at me, sometimes returning my wave of greeting. I did notice, on Sundays, the youth with the motorcycle who parked near the chapel railings, as the congregation left. Sometimes, I noticed the surreptitious glances or signs that passed between him and Irene, and felt sorry for the restricted life of this pleasant girl.

I had no idea how restricted it was until she halted one morning with tears in her eyes. I was sitting astride my machine, doing little more than while away five minutes before making a point at Maddleskirk Abbey telephone kiosk. Irene halted her bicycle in the manner adopted by so many lady riders – she didn't use the brakes, but allowed her left foot to scud along the ground until the bike was compelled to halt beside me.

I smiled.

'Good morning, Irene. How's that aunt of yours?'

I saw tears in the girl's eyes, and immediately wished I hadn't sounded so jovial.

'I don't care!' she said. Her calm face had a sullen pout and an air of utter misery.

'Something wrong?' I wondered why she had stopped to talk to me.

'I don't know who can help me,' she wept gently. 'I was always told by Aunt Sadie that policemen are there to help people ...'

'Yes, we are. If it's something I can help with, I'll be only too pleased to listen. Do you want to talk here?'

'There's nowhere else.' She wiped a tear from her eye. 'Besides, I mustn't be late.'

'Well,' I spread my hands in a gesture of openness, 'here I am.'

'It's Aunt Sadie,' she said. 'She ... well, Mr Rhea, she's so old-fashioned ... you see, I have met this boy ... and ...'

I finished the sentence for her, 'And she won't let you meet him?'

Irene nodded.

I continued, 'Is that the young man who comes on a Sunday, with his motorbike?'

'Yes, I'm not allowed out to meet him, you see, not at all, never. He sees me at work, when I make his coffee...'

She explained about the bread deliveries and I began to understand. She told of the tribulations in her sheltered life, and I felt very sorry for her. I began to wonder if Aunt Sadie was really the girl's mother, and whether Aunt Sadie had experienced some unfortunate love affair in her sheltered past ... perhaps this was her way of protecting this quiet girl from a similar fate?

I listened carefully, and realised it was beyond my powers; although I had every wish to see this girl happy and content, I felt it was not part of a policeman's duty to interfere with domestic arrangements. Yet I did not like to tell Irene this; she had come to me seeking help.

When she had finished her catalogue of sorrow, she said, 'And now, Mr Rhea,' then burst into a flood of tears, 'Andrew says he will not come to see me any more, not after chapel, and not for coffee … he'll bring a flask, unless I meet him after work, or take him home…'

'I can understand him saying that, Irene,' I said. 'He drives an awful long way just for a glimpse of you on Sundays, and if his only chat is over a quick coffee, with folks standing around, I'm surprised he's been so persistent and faithful to you. Many lads would have given up weeks ago.'

'Yes, I know, but he loves me, you see. He honestly does.'

'I don't doubt it for one minute, Irene. But have you told your aunt about him?'

'Told her? Oh, no, I daren't do that! She's never let me go out alone, and if she knew I had a boyfriend she might stop me going to work … she's very funny about boys…'

'You're telling me!'

'Mr Rhea, you must help me. Please. Can't you just ask her to let me see him?'

'It must have taken a lot of courage for you to approach me?'

'There's nobody at work, they'd just laugh at me. They don't understand. I thought about the minister at the chapel, but he's friendly with Aunt Sadie and, well, you are a policeman, aren't you?'

'Yes, I am,' I was thinking fast. 'Look,' I said, 'Will

you be at chapel this coming Sunday?'

'We never miss.'

'And Andrew? Can you persuade him to ride out once more?'

'I think so. Have you something in mind?'

'I was thinking. I have to see your aunt about a small query in that statement of hers. It's just a question of clarifying a small point. I could catch her outside the chapel on Sunday, and you could walk on and talk to Andrew. I'll discuss my point with her, and then I'll tell her what a nice lad you've found. I'll do my best to break the ice for you. How about that?'

Although my bland assurances cheered her immensely, I knew I was treading on very thin ice. If things went wrong, I could be blamed for all sorts, but I am a sucker for a pretty face with problems.

'Tell Andrew, won't you?' I said. 'If a policeman turns up when he's parked there, he might think he's going to get moved on or something. If he drives away, our plans will be ruined.'

She smiled and wiped away a tear. 'Yes, I'll tell him this morning.'

On Sunday, some twenty minutes before chapel was due to finish, I drove down the village in full uniform and parked near the railings. Andrew was already there. I removed my helmet, approached him and we shook hands. He impressed me as a very genuine lad, tall and confident with a head of carroty-coloured hair and a ready grin.

'Hello, you must be Andrew,' I said.

'And you are Mr Rhea. It's good of you to try this for us.'

'I only hope Aunt Sadie gives a little. You've an uphill battle there, young Andrew,' I warned him. 'She's a peculiar old thing, you know.'

'I know, Irene's told me all about her.'

I went over the plans and asked him to keep his fingers crossed. We occupied ourselves with small talk until the first of the congregation emerged. Aunt Sadie came out with Irene following closely, almost hiding herself as if to avoid the confrontation that must surely follow.

'Right, Andrew?'

'Yes, Mr Rhea,' and I walked away from him. 'Miss Breckon?' I called loudly for I wanted her to see me leaving this lad's presence; I wanted her to know I had been talking to him, the suggestion being that I knew him.

'Oh, Mr Rhea!'

'I'm sorry to bother you just after chapel, but I have a small point to clarify in your statement. I have it here ...' and I began to delve into my uniform pocket for the necessary papers.

Out of the corner of my eye, I saw Irene walk away from her aunt and move steadily towards the waiting Andrew. I kept her occupied. 'The problem is the car number you quoted,' I began, 'You said it belonged to the green Vauxhall, or the green car as you said, whereas both drivers state that the number you wrote down belongs to a tan car, a Hillman it was. Can we check it, please? You've got your piece of paper?'

This was the genuine enquiry which I was using to its ultimate; as I spoke, I saw Sadie's eyes follow Irene, so I said, 'I've just been talking to that young man. He's very nice and says he knows Irene from work.'

'She didn't tell me she knew any men!' she retorted.

'Oh, it's just an acquaintance,' I said. 'Do you mind if they chat while we check this number?'

She looked at Irene, now smiling at Andrew, and I knew I had confused her.

'Yes, you'd better come in, Mr Rhea. Irene,' she called, 'Dinner is at twelve.'

It was now half-past eleven. Was this a clear half-hour for Irene, or a reminder for the girl to come indoors and help with the preparation? But I strode inside with her and she had kept the piece of paper with the car number; it was tucked behind the tea caddy on the mantelpiece. She had written several snippets of information on it, and the car number was quite clearly recorded. It said 'green' beside it.

I saw Aunt Sadie screwing up her eyes as she tried to recollect the precise sequence of events, and then she said, 'No, you are right, Mr Rhea. The word 'green' refers to the driver's jacket. A green jacket, not a green car.'

'In that case, I'll need a supplementary statement to correct the first one. Can we do it now?'

She looked out of the window; Irene and Andrew were in full view; I had suggested this to him – 'Don't go out of her sight!' I'd warned him.

It took only five minutes to complete my formalities and I took my leave of her. The Sunday dinner was cooking and its lovely smell filled the kitchen.

'That smells good!' I said. 'You're making me feel hungry.'

'I believe in good food, Mr Rhea, and a good life,' at which she looked out of the window again.

'Miss Breckon,' I asked, following the line of her gaze, 'would you allow Irene to meet that boy again if she wanted?'

She looked at me steadily, and her eyes went moist, just a shade.

'If she must!' she stammered. 'But I want no trouble ... none. Not from lads ... I know what they can be ...'

'Perhaps if he always came when you were here too ...'

'Well, of course that would be all right. I mean, that's how things were done in the old days, before all this permissiveness. Girls introduced their beaux to their parents and there were always chaperones on hand ... besides, Mr Rhea, it is not the duty of a girl to invite a man to her home. It is the duty of the *man* to call and seek permission from the parents or guardians, if he wishes to escort a girl ...'

'If that young man called here, could he walk in the village with Irene?' I put to her, surprised at her old-fashioned views.

'I should consider it, Mr Rhea,' she said pertly.

'You will not be angry with Irene for talking to him alone, now?' I asked, tongue in cheek.

'No, if that young man is an acquaintance at work, then it would be discourteous to ignore him. I can see they are behaving in a perfectly proper way, and I have no objections.' She spoke rather stiffly, I felt, as she paid great attention to the old-fashioned rules of courtesy.

'Shall I tell Irene to come in when I leave?' I asked.

'I think the young man should make himself known to me,' she stated. 'I think that is his primary duty.'

I wondered where she had unearthed these Victorian ideas, but it seemed she was agreeable to Irene's courtship in condition it complied with those outmoded guidelines. How on earth Irene was supposed to know those old rules, or how Andrew was supposed to equate with them, was something they would have to learn for themselves. But the ice had been broken.

I left the house and walked over to them. Both smiled

at me, Irene with a definite look of apprehension on her face.

'She's fine,' I said, 'but she's living by some Victorian book of etiquette, I think. Andrew, this all depends on you. She will allow you to walk out with Irene, if you make a formal request. That means going to the house now, introducing yourself, and behaving like a gentleman of a bygone age. You must ask the guardian of Irene – that's Aunt Sadie – for permission to meet with her and walk with her. After that, you're on your own.'

'She'll see me now?' He seemed amazed.

'She's fine,' I said, 'but she's living in a different world from us. Once you can understand that, you'll get on with her. Right, get yourself over to that front door and tell Aunt Sadie who you are, where you are from, and tell her you'd like to escort Irene. That's how it used to be done.'

Irene smiled. 'Come along, Andrew, or should I call you Mr Pugh?'

'He's Mr Pugh for the time being!' I laughed, and left them to their new role. As I started my motorcycle and turned it around, I saw them crossing the road towards Aunt Sadie's red-brick house.

Next time I saw Irene, she stopped her bicycle and smiled at me. She looked relaxed and happy.

'That Sunday, Mr Rhea, well, Aunt Sadie invited Andrew to stay for dinner. She allowed him to walk me up and down the village because he'd knocked on the door and asked. We had Sunday dinner together, with her as chaperone. It was quite nice, and we all went for a walk in the afternoon.'

'So she was better than you thought, eh?'

'Mmm, much better. In fact, she's taken a liking to

213

Andrew. He can come every Wednesday evening and Saturday evening to walk about, and we can meet after chapel on Sundays. She says he can have Sunday dinner with us and we walk out in the afternoon.'

'Well, let's hope things work out for you. You're lucky to find such a nice lad, Irene.'

'I know,' and she blushed as she remounted her trusty bicycle and pedalled off to work.

Over the following few months, everything seemed fine with Irene and Andrew. He did not object to his visits being arranged and supervised by the watchful Aunt Sadie, and seemed happy to accept this as a condition for seeing Irene. I did not visit the house any more, although I would have welcomed an opportunity to view the entire premises. It was more like a Victorian museum than a modern household and as I passed from time to time, I noticed the aspidistras in the windows, and a pair of green witch globes dangling from a curtain rail. Truly, it was a house of the past.

But if the house and Aunt Sadie were relics from a past age, Irene and Andrew wanted to live and love in accordance with the norms of the twentieth century. This must have presented considerable difficulties and I wondered if Aunt Sadie abided by the words of Robert Browning when he wrote, 'All's love, yet all's law.'

But if Aunt Sadie's strict rules about love frustrated their lives, I have no doubt that the happy pair were fortified by words from Sadie's own Bible which said, 'Many waters cannot quench love, neither can the floods drown it.'

As the weeks passed from spring into summer, their friendship and love grew stronger. The virile Andrew, who must have been a man of infinite love and patience, wanted to spend some time alone with his Irene. And

Irene, being a blossoming girl, wanted to spend time alone with Andrew.

Aunt Sadie contrived to frustrate this event; she was a chaperone to beat all chaperones, one who could not be dodged or avoided, and one whose duties were clearly fixed in her old-fashioned head.

I wondered what the outcome would be; if Andrew had been any other modern youth, he would have ditched poor Irene weeks ago, not because of the girl but because of the overbearing supervision from Sadie. But his love never faltered.

At least, not until one evening in late September.

It was quarter to ten and the night was dark with the onset of autumn; there was a definite chill in the air, and the leaves were beginning to flutter from the trees. It was a clear night, however, with a full moon and small white clouds puffing their way across the sky. It was, beyond doubt, a night for romance. As my clock struck quarter to ten that Wednesday evening, I pulled my crash helmet over my head and prepared for my final tour of duty, a motorcycle patrol around my beat until 1 a.m. We called it half-nights; I'd been on duty since 5 p.m. and the patrol had been joyous, if peaceful and lacking in incident.

But as I made for the door after kissing Mary farewell, the telephone shrilled in the office. I hurried through, picked it up and heard the typical tones of a call from a kiosk. I waited as the caller pushed the money into the box. 'Aidensfield Police, P.C. Rhea,' I announced.

'Oh, Mr Rhea,' came the panting tones of a woman. 'It's my Irene and that Andrew, they've run away … you must find them … quickly.'

Although no name was given, I knew this was Miss

Breckon and said, 'I'll be there in one minute,' and hurried from the house.

By the time I arrived at the curious house, she had returned from the kiosk and was waiting in the front doorway where she was framed in the light of the interior. She was wringing her hands and fidgeting with anxiety.

She did not speak as I followed her inside and closed the door.

'Thank goodness I caught you!' she panted. 'Really, these young people … they are trying … and I thought he was such a nice young man …'

I removed my crash helmet and tried to calm her. I sat on the horsehair settee, and my action caused her to settle in a chair opposite.

'Now, Miss Breckon.' I spoke slowly and looked carefully at her. 'Let's start from the beginning. What's all this about Irene running away?'

'They've gone … both of them … on his motorbike…'

'When?' I asked.

'Just a few minutes ago …'

'Hold on,' I raised my hands, 'are you sure? Could they have gone for a spin in the moonlight? I see nothing sinister or worrying in a young man taking his girl for a motorcycle ride.'

'No, no … no, it's not like that, Mr Rhea, you must believe me … they've run away …'

'Miss Breckon, Irene is not a juvenile any more, nor is Andrew. He's over 21, and she is 19, and that means they can go for rides like this without the police being called in. If you're worried about her, then I could search – that's if you're really concerned for her safety, maybe thinking harm might befall her …'

I was trying in vain to make her understand that the police aren't concerned about girls of 19 having a quick cuddle or even going the whole way with their chosen boyfriends.

'No ... no ...' she was weeping now, 'they've run away...'

I paused, wondering what had prompted this drama, and said, 'Miss Breckon, what has happened?'

She did not reply immediately, but sat in the chair quietly allowing tears to run down her cheeks.

'They have run away,' she sniffed. 'She's gone ...'

'Was there an argument?' I sensed an atmosphere; it was difficult to define but something had happened between Aunt Sadie and the youngsters. Maybe the long-suffering Andrew had cracked at last?

She hung her head a long time before answering this question, and her lack of response told me the truth. There had been a dispute of some kind.

Finally, she said, 'Yes, Mr Rhea. I did remonstrate with them.'

'And they walked out?'

'Yes, and they went off on his motorcycle.'

'Can I ask what the argument was about?'

'I caught them misbehaving, Mr Rhea, in this house! I will not tolerate such behaviour, and I told them in no uncertain terms ... there are standards ...'

I held up my hand. 'Just a moment, how were they misbehaving?'

'I caught them in an embrace, kissing one another ...'

'Go on,' I wanted to hear this. It looked as if Andrew hadn't wasted his opportunity.

'Well, he came into the house this evening, Mr Rhea; he asked if he could speak to me and I allowed him in, in spite of the lateness of the hour.'

'And then?'

'He asked if he could take Irene home to meet his parents, on Sunday afternoon after chapel. He proposed to pick her up on his machine, take her to Scarborough for Sunday dinner, and return her in the early evening...'

'I think that is a perfectly normal thing – and it was good of him to seek your permission.'

'Well, Irene's never been to a big city like Scarborough ... anyway, Mr Rhea, I had once been to Scarborough, long ago, and my mother had some photographs of me near the Spa. I wanted them to see me there. Well, I went upstairs to find the album and in those few moments, he and Irene ... well ... they kissed and embraced ...'

'And you were angry?'

'I felt insulted; I felt let down. The moment my back was turned they started misbehaving ...'

'That is not misbehaving in a modern society,' I tried to explain but knew it was useless. 'Anyway, what happened?'

'Well, as I remonstrated with them, Andrew grabbed his things and rushed out, saying I was a stupid old woman ... and Irene ran after him ... then they disappeared on his bike and ...' she burst into a fit of sobbing. I felt sorry for her although this was of her own making.

'Miss Breckon,' I said firmly, 'domestic disputes of this kind are not a police matter. You ought to know that. Irene is old enough to go out with boys and I know she's a sensible girl and that she won't let you down ...'

'She has ... she kissed that ... that horrible youth ...'

I ignored this remark, as I continued, 'But because of your concern, I will radio my Control Room and ask our patrols to look out for Andrew's motorbike. It can't be far, and I will ask him to bring Irene back. The radio is on my motorcycle outside.'

I had little hope of finding Andrew and Irene, for it was impossible to know where they'd gone, but miracles do sometimes happen and within half an hour, the radio on my motorcycle alerted me and I responded. I learned that Andrew had been traced to a fish-and-chip shop in Eltering, but Irene was not with him. According to him, she had not left on his motorcycle; that was the message I received, and Control Room said that Andrew was now heading back to Aidensfield. The drama had produced an unexpected twist.

'This alters things, Miss Breckon,' I said. 'If she's not with Andrew, where is she?'

Her answer came in a flood of tears. 'I don't know, I don't know … I thought she'd gone with him … they went out … tore out … and I heard the motorbike go …'

This put me in something of a dilemma. All kinds of possibilities flashed through my mind – was Irene bent on committing suicide? Or was she running headlong into the night? Or had she gone for a quiet think somewhere? Maybe there was a friend in the village she wanted to talk to? What had been the last words between Andrew and herself? Should I begin a localised search, or did the circumstances justify a full-scale hunt? Girls in love were prone to acting in odd ways. The answer was that I did not know what to do – I believed she would return if we left her alone, but I could be wrong. There were so many imponderables.

'I think I'd better wait for Andrew,' I decided. 'I must hear what happened between them after they left the house.'

'You don't expect me to welcome that man back into my house, after desecrating my niece, do you?' Her eyes flashed at me.

'I'll speak to him outside,' I made a rapid compromise.

There followed an embarrassing silence, so I went outside and sat upon the saddle of my stationary motorcycle to await the return of Andrew Pugh. This also gave me the advantage of being able to look up and down the village street in case Irene decided to reveal herself before coming home.

The door remained open, and I could hear occasional movements of Miss Breckon inside, but she never emerged to enlighten me further about the events which precipitated this action. After nearly half an hour, Andrew arrived and parked near me. He hurried over, obviously very worried and said, 'What's happened, Mr Rhea? The policeman said Irene had run away.'

'We thought she was with you,' I said.

'Did she say that?' and he pointed at the house.

'She thinks it is true.' I spoke in defence of Miss Breckon.

'Silly old besom!' he spat. 'I've never come across anybody like her, honest. I lost my rag, Mr Rhea.'

'What happened? Can you throw any light on it for me? It might help us to find Irene. Where in the name of God do we start to look? I just don't know.'

'Well,' he put his crash helmet on the tank of my motorcycle, and loosened his jacket. 'You know what she's like?'

'I do,' I sympathised.

'I wanted to ask Irene over to our house next Sunday, so I knocked on the door and was invited in. So far so good. When I got on about Scarborough, she said she loved Scarborough and wanted to show us – me and Irene that is – some photos she'd had taken there years ago. So she went upstairs to find them. Well, Mr Rhea, I mean, that was the first time ... the first bloody time we'd been alone ... so I gave Irene a cuddle and a kiss. You know, arms round her waist and a kiss on the lips ... she responded ... we've been waiting for bloody weeks for just a few minutes like that, alone ...'

'And she caught you?'

'She's drilled bloody holes through the floor boards, Mr Rhea! Just you have a look. In that room, that living room ceiling which is all beams and floor boards, there's bloody great holes drilled through. Peep holes, all over, so anybody up there can peep down ...'

'You saw them?'

'I did! She had the light on up there, seeking her photos, and I looked up and caught her ... I saw this beady bloody eye staring down at us, and so I gave her the old two-fingers and gave Irene a right bloody snog!'

I laughed. 'You're not serious, Andrew?'

'Just you have a look next time you go into the room.'

'What happened then?'

'Well, she came storming downstairs and went berserk. She accused me and Irene of being immoral, said Irene was a slut and sex-mad and, well, I thought she'd blown a gasket. I lost my rag; I said I was standing no more of this and stormed out. I got on the bike, revved up and cleared off.'

'And Irene?'

'I dunno. I thought she'd be kept in.'

'You didn't look behind as you left?'

'Not likely. I was going to write to Irene, or see her in the kitchens tomorrow, just to say I loved her ... but that silly old ...'

'That's a new one on me,' I said, 'spy holes in the floor, but it seems Irene ran out after you. Obviously she didn't catch you and the old lady thought you'd both run off. Now, Andrew, think hard. Did you and Irene talk about anything that might give us a clue where to look?'

He thought hard. 'We talked about going for walks in the woods,' he said, 'if we were allowed to be alone. But wherever we went, away from the house, Aunt Sadie came. We talked about going walking alone, Mr Rhea, or going for a day out somewhere, like Whitby or across the moors.'

'Did she know any walks in this area?'

'Oh yes, apparently when she was little, she and Aunt Sadie would spend hours walking the woods and fields.'

'Had she a favourite?'

'Yes,' he pondered, 'yes, now you mention it. There's a place called Lover's Leap, where you can sit on a bench and look down a cliff into the river ... apparently two lovers jumped off long ago ...'

'God!' I swore. 'Andrew, could she have thought you were running out on her? I mean you roared off ... leaving her to face Aunt Sadie ... Now, if she thought you'd given her up ...'

'Where is this place?' he cried.

'I know it. Start your bike – I'll come with you on the pillion. I'll tell Sadie to stay here with the door open, in case Irene comes home.'

Minutes later, we were bumping along the footpath which ran beside the river, rising through the dense woodland with its beeches and oaks, and all the time keeping our eyes open for the fleeing girl. Andrew's driving was skilful on very narrow and difficult terrain, and his headlight picked out the trees, the rocks, the tumbling river with its rapids and black whirlpools. We did not speak, except when I guided him left or right as we roared towards the towering cliff known as Lover's

Leap.

'There she is!' Suddenly, I could see her on the rustic seat which overlooked the ravine through which the river ran.

'Irene!' Andrew shouted, 'It's me ...'

I don't know whether she could hear his voice above the roar of the river or whether the noise of the oncoming motorcycle unsettled her, but she stood up and began to walk towards the edge of the cliff.

'God Almighty!' he shouted, accelerating wildly. 'Look at her! Irene!'

Seconds later, he swept to a standstill before Irene, who stood in the moonlight in her summer dress with tears streaming down her face.

'Go!' I hissed in his ear, 'I'll look after the bike.'

I saw her fall into his arms as I kept my distance.

'I'll see you two back at the house,' I said, turning Andrew's motorbike around. 'It's a good hour's walk if you take your time.'

And I drove away.

Back at the house, Aunt Sadie emerged when she heard the motorcycle, and showed surprise when I clambered from it. I went indoors, and closed the door behind me.

'We've found her, and she's fine,' I told her. 'She's walking back with Andrew; they'll be about an hour. She'd gone for a long think about things.'

'Is she all right?' was her first question.

'Yes, she's fine,' I was pleased to tell her.

She walked into the living room and I found myself looking at the ceiling. Half-inch holes had been drilled through the floor boards in dozens of places, each giving a sneak view of anything that occurred below. She saw me examining them and began to cry.

'Andrew told me about the upset,' I said gently.

'I ... it wasn't me ... I didn't put those holes there,' she said. 'My mother did. She drilled them to spy on me ... and ... I daren't bring boyfriends in ... she watched us ... and ... well, it made me go all secretive ... and ...'

'You rebelled and have regretted it ever since?' I said.

'Mr Rhea, I'm sure you must know that Irene is my daughter, born late in life ... I knew nothing of life ...'

'But Irene will head the same way if you force her. You must see that ...'

'I do, I do ... I'm trying to protect her, and I do love her so, and don't want to see her harmed ...'

'Then trust her. You've got to win back her trust, haven't you, after tonight? She is a lovely girl, and she loves you,' I said. 'Now, she has found a boyfriend in a thousand, a real nice boy. Don't let her lose him, Miss Breckon. Let her go to Scarborough for Sunday lunch; let him stay here one weekend ... trust, Miss Breckon. It's needed on both sides. It is cruel not to trust,' I added, dragging part of a quote from Shakespeare to the forefront of my mind.

I remained with her, drinking a welcome cup of tea, until I heard the youngsters outside.

'It's time for me to go,' I said. 'Welcome them back, show them *both* you love them. Andrew is right for her, Miss Breckon, I'm sure of it.'

'He's good for us both, Mr Rhea.' She escorted me to the door, smiling, and opened her arms to welcome the young lovers.

Constable Around The Village

Life on the beat in rural North Yorkshire. How hard can that be for a young bobby?

PC Nick Rhea is about to find out that Aidensfield isn't the sleepy village it may seem.

Sheep-worrying, graveyard fights, missing men and a thieving bus conductress are just some of the problems he faces as he settles into village life.

And soon he learns that law enforcement in Aidensfield can be unofficial but still highly effective in this vivid and light-hearted insight into rural policing.

Out now
SBN 9781906373368
Price £7.99

Constable On The Prowl

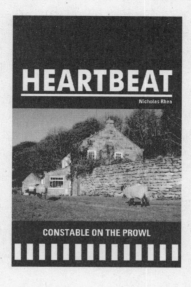

Young bobby Nick Rhea is settling into his new life patrolling the sleepy Aidensfield, but he still hates working nights.

Under the cover of darkness, Nick gets to know his colleagues. He also has his first encounter with local rogue Claude Jeremiah Greengrass, who is beating a hasty retreat from a lady's bedroom!

Practical jokes and friendship combine as Nick warms to life in the village he will soon *consider his home*.

Out now
ISBN 9781906373351
Price £7.99

Constable Across The Moors

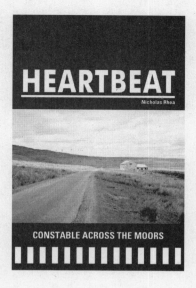

Police Constable Nick Rhea continues his heart-warming account of rural bobbying on the North Yorkshire moors and finds himself dealing with a host of intriguing characters who live and work on the wild moors.

In his latest adventures he investigates a case of witchcraft, which local lass Katherine Hardwick employs to rid herself of a troublesome suitor.

Then there's the strange story of the insurance man who covers a dog against its persistent theft, and unscrupulous love-making.

Published October 10th 2008
ISBN 9781906373375
Price £7.99

Constable Along The Lane

Crime comes to Aidensfield when haystacks are fired and Arnold Merryweather's ancient bus helps catch a car thief.

Rural bobby PC Nick Rhea gets more than he bargained for when he arrests a pig thief, and the pregnant pig, much to the annoyance of the police station cleaner!

But it's not all crime. A glider crashes into a thatched cottage and Nick also gets involved in a plot to force a Yorkshire miser to spend some money.

Published November 11th 2008
ISBN 9781906373405
Price £7.99

Constable By The Sea

During a seasonal break from his usual village beat on the North Yorkshire moors, young Police Constable Nick Rhea finds himself involved with holiday-makers and their problems.

As well as his normal seaside duties, how does he cope with a man who has lost his false teeth in the sea and another who wants to give away thousands of pounds, when drunk?

Then there's the stray Labrador that thinks he's a police dog and accompanies police officers on night patrols, and the anxious fisherman who daren't tell his wife that he owns a racehorse.

Published November 11th 2008
ISBN 9781906373399
Price £7.99